TRAINING MY HEART TO LOVE YOU

MONICA WALTERS

Introduction

Hello, Readers!

Thank you for purchasing and/or downloading this book. This body of work contains some hot, steamy sex scenes and vulgar language. There are also issues dealing with obesity and suicide. If any of that offends you, or serves as triggers for unpleasant times, please do not read.

If you are okay with the previously mentioned warning, I hope that you enjoy the ride this story takes you on. Have an open mind when you read and, remember, just because it may not be your reality doesn't mean that it isn't someone else's. Peace and love always.

Monica

Chapter One

K ortlynn

"IF WE DON'T EDUCATE OUR YOUNG GIRLS, WHO WILL? DO WE really want to leave that in the hands of the female rappers and Instagram models? When Ms. Taylor left me in charge of Integrity, she only made one request. That request was that I would teach these girls to have self-respect, to be self-sufficient and to know their self-worth. I won't let her, or them, down. So, let's get to work, planning for a great summer program."

When everyone left the conference room, I sunk in one of the plush chairs. I was so tired from the day's activities, I didn't know how I would make it home. I'd just finished my staff meeting for the girl's center I began running a couple of years ago. Things hadn't been great, because I'd been trying to learn the ropes. However, I planned to perform CPR on it, this summer, giving it life renewed. The name of the center was Integrity. This was the main virtue we wanted to teach the girls. If they had integrity, everything else would fall into place.

Serita Taylor was the owner and founder, but she'd taken an indefinite leave of absence. The program and the girls were in despair for a little over a year. The rumor was that she'd somehow gotten addicted to cocaine. I quickly dispelled that rumor, because I just couldn't imagine it. When she finally returned, she informed us that she would be stepping down, due to some personal demons she had to face, and would be closing the center. She was in no position to be a light to others when she couldn't find the light within herself. That spiel from her made me believe that the rumor was possibly true. Instead of closing it, though, I begged her to let me run it. So, she dropped everything in my hands and left.

That was a little overwhelming, being that I'd just gotten my master's degree in family counseling. I had no clue how to run a government-funded, non-profit program. The girls didn't seem to respect me as much as they did her and the other women that were involved. A lot of them were Ms. Taylor's family, so when she went MIA, so did they. It was tough around here for a while. Now that I, and my still fairly new staff, have gotten a handle on things, we were ready to revamp everything around this place. Plus, Ms. Taylor said she would be visiting from time to time, this year, to see how things were going. Everything was still in her name, so I could understand her concern, dealing with the government.

Grabbing my phone from my purse, I needed to call my cousin, Legend. He was a bull rider and had connections to all things country, so he was sure to be able to help me find the help I needed to implement a new program for the girls. Hopefully, he wasn't busy. Hesitantly, I found his number in my contacts. I really didn't like asking for help, but I knew I couldn't start this program on my own. "Hello?"

"Legend, hey! It's Kortlynn."

"What's up, lil mama?"

"Not too much. I was calling to see if you knew someone that wouldn't mind teaching the girls, at Integrity, how to garden. I've been around cement all my life, so there's no way I could help them with that."

He chuckled. "Hmm. Red has a friend that farms and trains horses. Let me find out if Zay would be willing to do that. Do you have an idea on the date?"

Red was Legend's wing man and a steer wrestler. It was like one couldn't function without the other in their careers. It was amazing how close they were and how they fed off each other. "I don't have an exact date, but sometime toward the end of next month."

"Aight. Let me call you back."

I ended the call, then gathered my things to go home. Had I sat there any longer, I was gonna end up spending the night. Taking my heels off and carrying them in my hand, I slid on my Nike slides and walked out to my car. The cool breeze blew through my curls, making me feel amazing. For a moment, it felt like the makeup was melting off my face and it was only April. I couldn't wait to get out of this skirt set, that made me look ten years older, and into something more comfortable.

Being a plus-sized woman already added age to me, according to my mother. I'd been a big girl most of my life and, unfortunately, that wasn't about to change no time soon. Although I was comfortable in my own skin and size eighteen clothing, I knew I needed to lose a few pounds. My knees and ankles were starting to give me some issues. The doctor had ruled out arthritis, a few months ago, and suggested that I start a workout routine or start walking. While I had no other health issues, I didn't need to be cripple either.

My apartment was only five minutes from Integrity, so, by the time my car cooled off, I was home. When I parked the car and made it inside, I literally had to sit down and cool off before going a step further. As I sat, soaking in the seventy-two-degree air coming from my a/c unit, my phone rang. Slightly rolling my eyes, I answered the call from Mary Hebert, my mother. "Hello?"

"Hello, Kortlynn. Are you already home?"

"Hello, Mom. Yes, I am."

"I was hoping you would have come by here today, but we can talk tomorrow."

"What about?"

"Don't worry. We'll talk about it tomorrow."

That let me know that it was probably about something I could care less about. After staying quiet for a moment, I said, "Okay. Well, I'll see you tomorrow."

"Okay. Your Aunt Rose is going to be here, tomorrow evening, getting measured. I'm making a dress for her to wear to a wedding."

Aunt Rose was Legend's mom. My mom was his mom's sister. You wouldn't be able to tell by the way they act, though. Aunt Rose was so down to earth, but my mama could be downright bougie. I didn't know why, since everyone knew her past. According to Aunt Rose, she'd tried to trap my dad by getting pregnant when she knew he didn't want kids or to be with her. She stopped her birth control and poked holes through all his condoms at her house. If that wasn't some hoe shit, I didn't know what it was. "Okay, Mom."

"Bye, sweetie."

"Bye."

Once I ended the call, then checked again to make sure she was indeed off my line, I said aloud, to myself, "Ugh! She gets on my nerves!"

I would never disrespect her and say that to her face. Her feelings get hurt easily and, despite everything, I knew she loved me. I loved her, too, and she was my mother. She'd ended up raising me alone, for the first ten years of my life, and she'd done an amazing job as a single mother. Whatever her past life may or may not have been, she'd always put me first. For that, I was grateful.

Finally getting up from the couch, I went to my bedroom to get out of my work attire. I had no plans for the night. Although the center was closed tomorrow, I would be there for a couple of hours, ironing out details of the gardening plan. It was to fit along with my self-sufficiency program for the girls. Being lonely was tough. I didn't have any close friends that I could hang out with, besides my cousin, J'Neka. She lived in Denton, now, because she was in a graduate program at North Texas. She would be home for the summer, in mid-May, and I couldn't wait.

Not only didn't I have close friends, but I didn't have any male companionship either. Guys I was interested in often put me in the friendzone or ignored me altogether. That was so disheartening. I stayed looking fly as hell, even in my business attire. My mama taught me how to be fashionable and, even though she stayed on me about my size, she helped me find clothes that flattered my figure. I had curves for days and my confidence was on ten, but nobody was biting. At the age of thirty-two, I just didn't understand it. I should have been attracting mature, grown ass men, but that wasn't the case.

Laying across the bed, in my bra, panties and waist trainer, I huffed loudly. My social life was pathetic, and I needed to start getting out more often. Besides going to work, and church on Sundays, the only place I frequented was the grocery store. After getting my waist trainer off, my phone began ringing. Snatching it from the bed, I saw it was Legend calling me back. "Hey, cuz."

"Hey, Kort. So, Red contacted Zay, and he said he wanted to look at the area he would be using to teach them before he committed. He doesn't want the ground to be inadequate. The crop needs to be successful, so it doesn't look like he failed them."

"Okay. When does he want to come? I'll be there tomorrow, but I can be there whenever he has time."

"Why don't I give him your number? That way I ain't gotta be the middleman."

"Okay. That's cool. Thanks, Legend. I appreciate it."

"No problem."

He ended the call, and I went to the bathroom to start the shower. Tonight, I would be researching the doctorate programs at Lamar University. I'd waited years before I went back for my master's degree, but if I found a degree program I was interested in, I would be starting in August.

After my shower was done, I began moisturizing my long legs. It was what I liked most about my five-foot-seven-inch frame, besides my lips. As I did, my phone began ringing. Not recognizing the number, I frowned. Then, I quickly remembered that Zay, Red's friend, would be calling. "Hello?"

"Hello. May I speak to Kortlynn Hebert?"

I wondered if he was from this area. People from this area always mispronounced my last name. It was pronounced A-bear. However, that shit wasn't important. What was of high importance was this sexy ass voice. I didn't know if I was just desperate as hell or if it was as sexy as I thought it was. It had the depth of Michael Clarke Duncan with a hint of raspiness. *Damn, calm your thirsty ass down, Kort.* "This is she."

"This is Zayson Ardoin. And my bad, but your last name is probably pronounced A-bear. I just read it from the text Legend sent."

"That's quite alright. It is pronounced A-bear."

"Okay. So, when can I come look at the area you want to garden?"

"Whenever it's convenient for you."

"I don't have any horses to train, right now, so I can come tomorrow."

"Great. I'll be there. What time did you want to come?"

"Will ten be okay?"

"Sure. The center is on Highway 105, near Major Drive. The address is 7680."

"Okay. I'll see you at ten, Ms. Hebert."

"Call me Kortlynn. Ms. Hebert is my mother. Thank you so much."

He chuckled. *Damn.* "Okay, Kortlynn. Bye."

"Bye."

My Lord. I fell back on the bed, my heart beating fast as hell. There was no way I was wearing business attire tomorrow, but Sista Big Bones was going to be fly as hell.

Chapter Two

Z ayson

"HE READY. WHEN YOU GET READY TO SLIDE OFF HIS ASS, TO catch that steer, you gon' see. He'll work the rope real nice for you, too, if you decide to tie down off of him."

"Aight. I'm gon' put him to the test, when I get home. Thanks, Zay."

Gerald was a steer wrestler, primarily, but he also roped calves. We called calf roping tie down, because, once the calf was roped, the rider jumped off the horse to tie three of his legs together. Usually, different horses were used for the different events, but I had to let him know how talented this one was. I participated in the rodeo, for a couple of years but, when I got hurt, I gave it up. It wasn't a bad injury, just a bruised ACL. However, the big bucks hadn't started rolling in yet, so I couldn't risk not being able to make a living. I was still working a regular job, at the time, for Lower Neches Valley Authority, maintaining canals as a crew leader. I hated that damn job.

Now, the only jobs I had were training horses for rodeo events and breaking the wild ones so they could be ridden. Sometimes, I sold crops from my farm and hay from my field, but the horses kept my money right, especially since my buddy, Red, had been rodeoing more. He'd passed his customers to me, because he just didn't have the time. He was big shit, now, in steer wrestling. He and Legend had turned the world on to black cowboys and that shit made me proud.

Legend had called earlier about his cousin needing someone to help her show some lil girls how to garden. I really didn't feel like doing the shit, but I needed to give back. Living in China, Texas, keeping to myself and stacking my paper, wasn't benefitting nobody but me. My mama was on me hard about settling down with a nice woman and all that family bullshit. I was thirty-four years old and had been bitten by love too many times to count. None of that shit lasted, so I chose to stay to my damn self and concentrate on what was important to me. My money.

When I called her, her voice caught me off guard. It was so smooth and sexy. She was speaking in a lower register like India Arie. I had to remind myself that I wasn't fucking with nobody like that, right now, and to calm my horny ass down. Beating off in the shower was getting old, but women didn't know how to keep their damn feelings to themselves when they got the dick put to 'em right. I hadn't come across a female that made me wanna risk it yet, so he was just gon' have to settle for the beating he was gonna get tonight.

I just hoped like hell that Kortlynn wasn't attractive. My type varied, but one thing I didn't really go for was a skinny chick. I preferred to have something to grab on to. Hell, I wasn't fat, but I was kinda thick my damn self and being six-foot-five, I'd break her ass. Big girls loved the hell out of me, but I had yet to meet one that caught my attention. They were usually too forward. I'd have to say, "Like, damn. Listen. Let me chase *you*." That was an immense turn off for me. So, I would find out about Kortlynn in the morning.

Before I could get in the house good, my mama was calling. "What's up, Ma?"

"Zay, your daddy said that Kerry bought a racehorse. I know like hell he didn't do that shit."

I chuckled to myself. Kerry was my older brother that acted like he was still a damned teenager. "Yeah, Ma. He bought it yesterday, I think."

"Why you didn't try to talk him out of that fuckery?"

"He'd already bought it when he told me. I think he knew we would try to talk him out of it."

"If he ain't got nothing to do with his money, he can give that shit to me. That was a fucking waste."

"Ma, it's his money."

"You right. It is his money. But that muthafucka ain't paid us back none of the money he borrowed when he didn't have a job. His ass done caught amnesia. That was a loan until he got on his feet, not a got damn gift."

She was hot as shit. My mama cussed, but she rarely dropped the f bomb. She had my damn voice on pause. "Since his ass won't answer my calls, when you talk to him, tell him I want my fucking ten grand, since he can afford a racehorse."

She ended the call, like I was the one that had pissed her off. During our childhood, she did that shit all the time. When one of us got in trouble, the other one had better stay the hell out her way. I wondered how Daddy found out Kerry had bought a racehorse, because I knew he wasn't happy about that shit either. They shouldn't be surprised that Kerry ain't done what was right. That nigga been that way his whole life. It was like we weren't even raised by the same parents.

After taking my shower, I sat and ate some left over baked ribs, greens and scalloped potatoes that my mama had cooked for me. She was forever looking out for me. But I always looked out for them, too. My daddy had some health issues, so I made sure their grass was cut and that shit was running right around their house. I was good with my hands and was just naturally good at fixing shit. Kerry was always on the receiving end, but never wanted to give even his time to spend with them.

I exhaled, thinking about the predicament he could have possibly gotten himself into. He'd borrowed the money from a fucking loan shark. This nigga borrowed seventy grand for a damned horse. Ain't no way in nobody's fucked up world should he have done that shit, whether he owed anybody else money or not. If that horse didn't perform like it should, he would be stuck paying that shit back. Kerry didn't know shit about racehorses. He was letting this man gas him up into believing that he had bought the next winner of the Kentucky Derby. I hoped that muthafucka was right.

My mind then drifted to my meeting with Ms. Kortlynn. I was wondering how big the area was. If that soil was hard, but the area was small enough, she could buy the soil. But if it was too large of an area, this may be a project she may have to wait until next year to do, while they got the soil right. I was almost sure it would be fine, though.

Going to my room, my phone chimed, alerting me of a text message. Looking at it, I saw Red's picture. When I opened the message, it read, *I heard you going meet Legend's cousin, Kortlynn, tomorrow.*

I answered immediately, *Yep.*

Well, she thick. You know how you feel about that. Just thought I would prepare you.

Aww fuck. Just what I needed. *How thick? Thick with a flat stomach or thick, thick.*

Thick, thick. And fly as hell.

Great. I sent him the smh emoji, then laid in the bed. I didn't know how I would go to sleep now, thinking about that shit. Then, he made it worse. He sent a fucking picture from her Facebook page. This chick had on some fishnets, a black shirt that read "size fabulous" and a metallic looking skirt. She was gorgeous. I had to stare at her picture for a while, because I wanted to memorize her every feature. Getting caught ogling her tomorrow, wouldn't be a good look. Those thick lips and big ass titties were pulling me in, not to mention those thick thighs and beautiful brown eyes.

When I finally had her image committed to memory, I laid down to go to sleep. That shit didn't last long, though, because my phone started ringing. Kerry. Here we go. "Hello?"

"You told Mama and Daddy about the racehorse?"

"Nope. Mama called me earlier, charging me up about it, wondering why I didn't tell them or try to stop you from doing it."

"You sure you didn't let it slip, when you were, maybe, talking to somebody else?"

"Nigga, you ain't that special for me to be talking about like that. Secondly, we live in China. It's only two-point-five people out here. Everybody know everybody business."

"I guess you right about everybody knowing everybody business. And I am that special."

"If you say so. You special alright."

"Whatever, Zay."

"Yeah. Let a nigga get some sleep. I'll holla tomorrow."

"Aight, bruh."

Finally, I could get some sleep. Maybe, if Kortlynn Hebert stopped plaguing my thoughts.

Chapter Three

⁂

K ortlynn

I was sitting at my desk, trembling in anticipation. Zayson Ardoin would be here, today, and I was nervous as hell. I didn't know what I was thinking wearing this long-sleeved shirt with these gray and white polka dotted, high-waisted pants. Sweat was gonna consume me before he even got here. I chose to get here at nine, thinking I would relax, but just the opposite was happening. The closer it got to ten, the more antsy I got.

After going to the restroom and walking out to the corridor, I saw a man that had to be at least six-foot-four-inches get out of a Dodge pickup. My God. This man was so damned fine, I had lost all train of thought. I'd been nervous for a reason. *Calm down, Kort. His type never falls for a woman like you.* However, that thought wasn't gonna keep me from serving him all this sex appeal. Those tattoos were about to take me down. Even though I didn't have any, seeing them on a man always took me there, and this brother had them all over his arms and probably all over his chest, too.

I walked toward the door to open it for him. He was wearing a green polo shirt that looked amazing against his skin, that was the color of a chai tea latte. That light brown complexion was mesmerizing and looked to have been kissed by the sun. I put an extra sway in my hips, as I approached the door and, when he looked up and saw me, it looked like he was just as mesmerized as I was. He licked his lips, as I unlocked it, and I avoided those sexy brown eyes, at all costs. I'd already noticed the freckles across the bridge of his nose. That meant I was staring too damn hard.

I opened the door. "Hello, Mr. Ardoin."

"Well, that ain't fair. If I get to call you Kortlynn, then you can call me Zayson or Zay."

He held his hand out to shake mine. Once I slid my hand in his, it felt like my insides melted. I smiled, then said, "Okay, Zayson. Thank you for coming. Follow me and I'll show you the area that I wanted to use."

He held his arm out and said, "Lead the way."

He was not what I was expecting. I wasn't a short woman, at all, but he made me look short as hell. I should've known better, though, if he hung with Red and Legend. This dude looked more urban than country. *Lord, please breathe on me.* I needed a cool breeze to sweep through this center right quick. As we silently walked through the hallway, I could see him looking around. "This place is nice."

"It really is. The founder put her everything into this place."

When I got to the back door, that led out to the area I wanted to use for the garden, Zayson stepped in front of me. "Let me get this door for you."

"Thank you." I walked through it, as my damn knees knocked. "So, what do you think about this area?"

He looked up in the sky, as if gauging the sunlight, then stooped to the ground and pulled up some grass, digging his fingers in the dirt.

"Well, the ground isn't hard and it's on the right side of the building, to where it would get plenty of sunlight."

He looked at the building and saw a waterspout against a wall and nodded his head. Damn, he was so fine. He wasn't skinny, but he wasn't overweight either; large enough to handle a big girl like me, though. As I drooled over his brown hair, tattoos and defined biceps, he turned back to me, causing those short sleeves to really strain against his arms. His goatee framed his mouth perfectly, as he smiled at me. Damn it, I felt activity below. "This location is perfect. You sure you don't know nothing about gardening?"

I giggled. "No. That was definitely a coincidence. Legend will tell you that."

He chuckled with me. "So, if it's okay, I wanna do a test run. Maybe one day, next week, come out and plant something to see how the ground takes to it."

"Oh. Okay. Just call to make sure someone is here."

He nodded, then led me to the door and opened it for me. "Thank you."

Once we were inside, I had him follow me to my office. After handing him a baby wipe to clean his fingers, I said, "Please have a seat, Zayson. We need to discuss your rates."

"What?"

"Your rates. Umm... I wasn't expecting you to do this for free. Legend told me you're pretty busy."

"Naw. I planned to volunteer my time. When he told me what type of program this was, I knew that I wouldn't be charging for this."

I had to have looked like a deer caught in headlights, the way I was staring at him. He chuckled, then leaned across my desk and grabbed my hand. What in the hell did he go and do that shit for? "I would be honored."

He released my hand. "Wow. Thank you. I'm in shock, somewhat. Please forgive me."

"Why are you shocked?"

"Well, you don't know me, and you probably hadn't heard about this program, until Legend told you about it. There are people that could donate that benefit directly from what we have to offer and don't give the first penny. So, I learned not to expect much financial help from the community."

"That's sad."

"Yeah."

He stood from his seat, so I stood from mine and stretched out my hand for a handshake. "Thank you so much, Zayson. I really appreciate this."

He smiled, as he shook my hand. *Damn.* I averted my gaze to the papers on my desk as I pulled my hand away from him. Following behind him to the door, he stopped abruptly, and I almost ran into the back of him. He turned to face me, and I nearly stopped breathing. "This might be unprofessional as hell, but umm... can I take you to lunch?"

"You want to take *me* to lunch? I should be taking you."

He smiled again and I knew I had creamed in my panties that time. Watching him lick his lips didn't help the situation. He held his hand out for mine, so I leaned over to grab my clutch, then put my hand in his. My God, the warmth. As he led me out of my office, I closed and locked the door. "So, how long have you been working here?"

"I've been here for almost ten years. I became the director, about three years ago."

"That's cool. You look too young to be a director."

I giggled. "So, how old should a director be?"

"Thirty plus."

I looked at him in awe. For him to say that went against everything my mama said. "So, out of curiosity, how old do you think I am?"

"Aww, shit. I probably set myself up just now."

I giggled more as we walked out the entrance and I locked the door. "I'm not setting you up. I promise. My mother always says I look older than what I am, so I'm intrigued."

"Aight. Well, let me see."

He grabbed my hand and spun me around, making me heat up under his careful observation. "Okay. I'm gonna say you about twenty-eight."

"You not tryna kiss up or earn a favor from me, are you?"

He laughed loudly, as I stared at him. Just 'cause I was lonely didn't mean I was naïve. Plus, I realized my professional tone had gone straight out the window. "That proper tone went right to hell. I like that, though. I ain't tryna kiss up. I'm a straightforward dude. You look about twenty-eight, for real."

"Well, I'm thirty-two, so I guess I'm qualified."

"Damn. You look good."

He opened the door to his truck and, for the first time ever, I became self-conscious. Probably because my ass would be in his face, as I stepped on the running board to get in the truck. Zayson placed his hands at my waist and helped me up, then closed the door. *Oh, my God. Please let me know, soon, if this is a test or a blessing, 'cause my heart can't take it.*

He hopped in the truck and started it. "Thank you, Zayson."

"For what?"

"For saying I look good and for lunch."

He waved his hand. "You thanking me for lunch and we ain't even got lunch yet. Where you wanna go?"

"Clearly, I'm not picky. So, it doesn't matter."

His face was extremely serious. It wiped the damn smile off my face. *What did I do?* "Listen. I know we just met, but I don't like you insulting or cracking jokes on yourself. That's not cool."

My lips parted and I wanted to kiss him. "I'm... umm... I apologize."

I was comfortable with him, up until now. Being that he was friends with Legend and Red, I may have gotten too comfortable too fast. Remaining quiet, I watched the scenery through the window, occasionally glancing at him. The nervousness was back. I joked a lot, about my weight, to make other people comfortable around me. I wasn't insulting myself. It was a fact that I wasn't a picky eater. Since high school, I'd always crack the joke before anyone else could. I guess it was a habit I needed to break.

Zayson drove into the parking area of a place called Amelia Farm & Market. I wasn't sure exactly what this place was, but I remained quiet. When he parked, I could see the picnic tables outside as well as an inside diner. Before I could open the door, Zayson grabbed my hand. "I didn't mean to make you uncomfortable, but you cracking jokes like that makes me uncomfortable. You're a gorgeous woman and this body is one to brag about."

This has to be a blessing. "Thank you, Zayson. It's always been a habit for me to crack the joke before anyone else could. Not because I have low self-esteem, because I know that I'm gorgeous. But, if I could make the joke, it usually made people more comfortable around me. I do apologize for making you uncomfortable."

"If your size makes people uncomfortable, they aren't worthy of being in your presence. Plus-sized women, especially one as beautiful as you, make me anything but uncomfortable."

He kissed my hand, then hopped out the truck. I could have melted in these seats. The last thing I was expecting from him was a mutual attraction. He made me glad that I chose myself over all those unworthy jackasses, in my past, that only wanted sex behind closed doors, but friendship in public. I was grateful my mother instilled self-love in me at a young age, so I wouldn't fall for the shenanigans and games those bastards wanted to play.

Zayson opened my door, but as I was getting out, I noticed how much attention he'd gotten already from the lil white girls around here. He probably had to fight them off with a damned stick, as fine as he was. As I lowered my heel to his running board, I slipped, nearly busting my ass, but Zayson, with the quick hands, wrapped his arm around me and lifted me like I didn't weigh shit instead of the two hundred forty pounds I was rocking. Now, that was embarrassing. "You okay?"

"Yeah. I don't think my heel is, though."

"Damn. My bad. Maybe we should have come in your car."

"That's not your fault. I was distracted."

"Yeah?" he asked, as he licked his lips. "What had you so distracted, Kortlynn?"

"This good-looking brother, about six-foot-four, light skinned with freckles and an amazing smile."

"Well, damn. You looking at another nigga while you with me?"

I laughed so hard, I almost slipped again. Zayson laughed, then picked me up from the running board and sat me on my feet. The way he slid me down his body, though, had my nipples hardening. "You are so silly."

He smiled at me. "And you are so beautiful."

My face heated up. "Thank you."

"Now, come on. Let's go eat some of this good food. You wanna sit inside?"

"Yes, please. I don't think the sun would get along too well with my makeup."

"Naw, probably not."

My heel was broken, but not bad enough to where I couldn't walk on it. We slowly made our way inside, and were sat at a table. Without perusing the menu, I knew what I wanted. He was sitting right in front of me.

Chapter Four

Z ayson

EVERY GOT DAMNED THING I SAID I WASN'T GON' DO, I DID. Kortlynn was so got damned beautiful, I needed more time just to stare at her fine ass. That picture Red sent me didn't do her justice. She was so mesmerizing, I couldn't keep my eyes off her. From the time she unlocked that door, at the girls' center, until now, she had my undivided attention. That shit was rare. I fought that shit until I couldn't anymore, because, as soon as I saw her, I wanted to say, *damn, baby girl, marry me*. All that flowing hair... shit, I could imagine it tousled and all over my pillows, after fucking the shit out of her.

The minute I touched her, I wanted to pick her up and have my way with her. That was some strong shit and I hadn't felt that in a long time. I could tell that she didn't play games and I liked that shit, especially when she asked me if I was kissing up to her. That proper tone went right out the window. However, when she cracked the joke about herself, it completely turned me off. When she explained why, I understood. Nothing was worse than being with a woman that lacked confidence. By the way she was dressed today, and the way she was dressed in the picture, I'd made the assumption that she was extremely confident, and I was glad to know that, once she declared how beautiful she was, that assumption was correct.

As she sat across from me, at Amelia Farm & Market, I wanted to pull her on top of that table and get my fill of her. She'd been blushing since we'd gotten here, and she'd done so a couple of times at the center. When she acknowledged that she was feeling me, too, I wanted to kiss those lips. And her laugh, the way she threw her head back, had me wanting to lick her neck. After ordering a Nut Pig Cuban, which was pastured pork, basil mayo, swiss and mustard on a ciabatta roll, she ordered the Figgy Piggy. I frowned up and looked at the menu again. When I saw it, my eyebrows lifted. "Yoooo, let me get that instead, too," I said to the waitress.

"Girl, all we gon' be able to do after this is take a nap. Ham, fig preserves and swiss cheese on a sour dough bun? Shiiiid, I'm gon' be damn near dead after this."

She giggled, trying to contain her laughter, in this restaurant. I reached across the table and grabbed her hand, just staring at her. She started to blush again, then looked down at our hands. "Why are you blushing so much?"

She smiled, then looked up at me. "You're making me blush, Zayson. I'm flattered. Extremely flattered."

That made me wonder just when the last time was that she'd gone on a date or, hell, just been complimented by a man. "So, after we leave here, what's on your agenda?"

She shrugged her shoulders. "I have to go to my mother's house, before I go home. That's about it."

"You like horses?"

"They're okay, I guess. I've never ridden one."

"What? You for real?"

"Yeah. Although Legend and I are cousins, we rarely went there to visit. They usually came to us. So, even as an adult, I rarely go out there and, when I do, it's to see Aunt Rose, his mother."

"Do you mind if I tried to help you change that? I have a ton of horses and I'd love for you to come ride, one day."

She bit her bottom lip. See, she was making my mind go there. This horse in my pants hadn't been mounted in a while and he was getting antsy. I shook my head slowly. "I could come one day."

And every day after that. The waitress brought our meal and both of our eyes widened at the size of that damned sandwich. "I already know I ain't gon' eat all this. Can you bring me a box?"

"Me, too, please."

After saying our grace, I took the first bite and it was everything I thought it would be. My eyes closed for a second as Kortlynn giggled. She smashed hers some, then picked it up and took a bite, doing the same thing I'd done. When she opened her eyes, she covered her mouth with her napkin. "This is so good."

"I know. This is it, right here."

After we enjoyed the rest of our lunch, we made our way back to Integrity, so she could get her car. My phone started ringing, with a call from Red, as we sat at the red light. I ignored the call, then proceeded to the center. Once there, I helped her out. Pulling out my phone, I put my arm around her shoulders, and she posed with her hand resting on my chest. I could see that I was gonna have to keep my distance when I was around her. She had me wanting to bust through these damn jeans. I took the picture, then she tiptoed to hug me. "Thank you so much for lunch."

Damn, she smelled good. "Thank you for accompanying me."

I handed her the leftovers she was leaving in my truck, then asked, "Is it cool if I call you sometimes?"

"Of course. I look forward to talking to you."

After flashing me a beautiful smile, she walked the short distance to her car. *Damn.* All that shit I put myself through last night and this morning, only to fall at her feet was amazing to me. She had that kind of power over a nigga. I was usually in control of my feelings and emotions but, in her presence, I couldn't even control the shit that came out of my mouth. Once she'd gotten in her car, she waved at me. I waved back, then got in my truck and sent Red the picture we just took.

Within seconds, he was calling me back. "Hello?"

"Nigga, damn! Y'all ain't waste no time, huh?"

"It's just a picture, Red. But, naw. I took her to lunch. We had a good time, and pretty much revealed that we were feeling each other."

"That's what's up. I was calling to see how it went."

"I knew that. That's why I didn't answer. We were still together."

"Wait 'til I tell Legend that Kort done got her a country nigga."

I laughed and shook my head. "Yeah, and I'm gon' have a citified chick."

"Now, just the fact that you gon' have a chick, at all, is the real story. I ain't really seen you messing around with anybody for like the past year. And shit, before that, it wasn't nothing serious."

"That was by choice, but after meeting her, I couldn't help myself."

"Shiiiid, nigga. I see."

We laughed and talked a little longer, until I got back to China. The minute I ended the call, my mind thought about the beautiful woman I'd spent time with today. I didn't want to leave her presence, but I couldn't sound all whipped already. Taking a deep breath, I turned in my parents' driveway to see Daddy trying to trim the hedges. After putting my truck in park, I sat there, watching him, while shaking my head slowly. He was so damned hardheaded. I told him when I cut the grass this evening, I would trim the hedges. It was the hottest time of the day.

I got out the truck and slammed the door, so he would look at me. He smirked, then sat the hedge trimmer down. "Man, what'chu doing?"

"Minding my business."

"Oh, yeah, old man? You are my business. Where Mama at?"

"She went to Beaumont, to go to the store."

"Oh, so you ain't had no supervision. What if you woulda passed out in this heat? I'ma tell Mama."

"Snitch."

"Bring yo' ass in that house."

When we got inside, I called Mama, while he sat there looking like a defiant kid. "You talk to yo' brother?"

"Hello to you, too, Barbara. Next time you leave, take yo' big ass kid with you. He can't be left unsupervised."

"What the hell you talkin' 'bout, boy?"

"Yo' husband was outside trimming hedges."

"Tell my overgrown son I'm gon' beat his ass when I get home. All them circulation issues, blood clots and shit we had to watch him go through, and he just gon' risk it all. I'll be there in ten minutes."

"Aight."

"You know, you and yo' mama just alike. All bark and no bite."

"Well, we gon' see. She said she was gon' beat yo' ass when she got here."

He rolled his eyes and I chuckled. "Daddy, it's not that we don't want you doing anything. Just make sure somebody is here, in case something happens. You out here, in ninety-degree weather, cutting hedges. I don't even wanna be out there right now. That's why I said I would do it this evening. It's hot as shit."

"Yeah. Aight, aight." He took a deep breath, then sat back in his recliner and put his feet up. "How did your meeting go today?"

"Good. Good as hell."

He looked over at me. "How so?"

"The director fine as hell."

He shook his head. "I should've known it was about a woman. When you gon' slow down?"

"Daddy, if I slow down, it'll be because of her ass."

I showed him the picture on my phone. He nodded, as he raised his eyebrows. "She's beautiful, son. What's her name?"

"Kortlynn Hebert. She's Legend Semien's cousin."

"Okay. Well, if she's that special, I'm almost sure I'll be meeting her soon."

I nodded my head, as he gave me the phone back. I stared at our picture and, I had to admit, we looked good together. "Zay!"

"Sir?"

"Aww, shit. You got it bad already. I called your name twice."

I waved my hand at him as Hurricane Barbara burst through the door. The chuckle left me before I could stop it. She stormed in the room. "Henry! I know yo' ass wasn't outside in this heat!"

"I wasn't. I don't know why baby boy lying on me."

My eyebrows shot up. "Nigga!"

He laughed and I couldn't help but join him. "I'm glad yo' ass think this shit funny, Henry. From now on, when I move, yo' ass move. Just like that."

"Ma, what you know about Ludacris?"

"Shut up, Zay. You ain't out the hot seat. You know you your brother's keeper."

"Ma, unfortunately, it ain't shit I can do about it now."

"You can convince him to sell that shit."

"Since when Kerry listen to me?"

She rolled her eyes. "Well, when you gon' bring a woman around here? I'm tired of y'all niggas."

"We may not have to wait too long, Barbara. Show her the picture, Zay."

I just stared at him. If I wanted to tell Mama, I would've told her already. She didn't know how to act sometimes. I already knew she was gon' be pressing a nigga to make a move now. "What you waiting on? Give it here, boy!"

I held the phone out to her, and she snatched it from me. "Oooh. She's gorgeous, Zay. Bring her to dinner, tomorrow, after church."

"See, that's why I don't tell you nothing. We just met today."

"This picture don't look like y'all just met today. If she doesn't have plans, bring her tomorrow. I'm gon' cook a big dinner just for the occasion."

I cut my eyes at my daddy as he chuckled. That was his way of getting me back. Mama handed me my phone and walked to the kitchen, as my daddy mumbled, "It don't feel good to be snitched on, huh?"

I rolled my eyes. "I'm going home and change. I ain't gotta stay here and take this abuse."

I stood from my seat. "And you betta have that young lady wit'chu tomorrow!"

"Bye, niggas!"

These two were about to drive me crazy. They were laughing extra hard when I walked out the door. I couldn't help but smile, though. After getting in my truck, to go home and change to come back and cut grass, I sent Kortlynn a text. *Do you have plans tomorrow?*

I rolled my eyes as soon as I sent it. My mama was serious as hell. She probably wouldn't let me eat at their house until I brought Kortlynn with me. My phone chimed. It was a reply from Kortlynn. *Not unless you do.*

I smiled, then told her to call me when she could. She wanted to be with me as badly as I wanted to be with her, and I appreciated that she wasn't about the games. We were too old for that shit, anyway. By the time I got in my driveway, she was calling. "Hello?"

"Hey, Zayson."

"Hey. Umm... I don't know how to say this, without sounding all soft and shit, but I showed my mother our picture. Now, she probably won't let me come back over without you. She wants you to come to Sunday dinner, tomorrow."

"Why would that make you sound soft? Send me the picture. I told my mama that I met someone I was interested in today. I just didn't have a picture to show her. What time is dinner? I go to church at nine-forty-five."

"We go to church at eleven, so after that. Around one or one-thirty."

"Zayson, if I'm being clingy, let me know. But, umm... could I go to church with y'all?"

Clingy? I didn't mind a woman being clingy, if I wanted her with me anyway. I sent her the picture, then responded. "Sure. We go to church right here in China, at St. Paul, but you can meet me at my house, and we can ride together."

"Okay. I'm excited. I feel so comfortable with you and that's unusual for me. I'm always on guard for foolishness, when it comes to men. Showing my excitement so soon after meeting you, is really baffling me."

"We in the same boat, then."

"Whatever!"

She laughed. "Naw, for real. I'm not usually as laid back either. And, to want to see you again, so soon, is almost unheard of. That doesn't happen hardly at all."

"So, what is it about me?"

"You're so cool. You're smart and sexy as hell. I can't seem to resist you. After hearing your voice, I wanted more."

"You, too, huh? I thought about you all night, last night."

"Damn, girl. Well, I can't wait to get to know you more. I have to cut some grass at my parents' house, in a lil bit, so I'll call you when I get back home and shower."

"Okay. My mom is looking at me sideways for being on the phone."

I chuckled. "Aight. Bye."

She called me while she was still at her Mama's house and said all of that on the phone in front of her. That spoke volumes to me. Within a matter of hours, we were ready to put one another first. Simply amazing.

Chapter Five

K ortlynn

"Kortlynn, this is Isaiah. He's a personal trainer at Exygon and can help you with getting some of the weight off."

I was stunned into silence. I couldn't believe she'd done some embarrassing shit like this. After ending my phone call with Zayson, and I'd shown her the picture, she'd said, "Oh. He's nice looking."

Then, someone had rang the doorbell and she came back with this guy. "Hello, Ms. Kortlynn. It's so nice to meet you."

He extended his hand and I hesitantly shook it. My mother, of all people, knew I didn't like being put on the spot. "Have a seat," my mother said as I cut my eyes at her.

This guy had a portfolio and was asking me all kinds of questions about my weight loss plan. I was silently fuming. Doing my best to tune him out, I began thinking about my conversation with Zayson. I should've gone with him today. Had I known I was gonna be ambushed, I would have. "So, what do you think about the plans, Ms. Kortlynn?"

"Let me look over them. I had no intentions of really starting a regimented program because, sometimes, I don't have the time to stick to it."

"I understand, Ms. Kortlynn. My card is in the portfolio. If you need my services, please don't hesitate to call."

I nodded, then stood to shake his hand. The minute he walked his ass out that door, I turned on Mary Hebert. "Before you come at me, you told me you wanted to lose weight and that you needed to get on a routine."

"Yes, I did! But you could have asked me before making him waste his time coming here. I don't have time for a program like that. My plate is full. My only days that I actually have that kind of time is on the weekends."

I grabbed my keys from the countertop, and was heading for the door, when my mother grabbed my arm. "I'm sorry, Kortlynn. I didn't mean to offend you. I was only trying to help."

"Mom, you knew I would be offended, that was why you didn't want to tell me what you had planned. It's okay, though."

She let me go, then watched me walk out the door. I was so angry, there was no way I could continue to sit there. I didn't want to disrespect her, even though she'd disrespected and offended me. For the first time, in a long time, my feelings were hurt, and I felt inadequate. Once I got in my car, I took a deep breath, pulled down my visor and looked at myself in the mirror, repeating the affirmations I said to myself daily. "Kortlynn Hebert, you are more than enough. You are gorgeous and your spirit is genuine. Your bodily housing has to be big to hold your heart, your loyalty, your trustworthiness and your intelligence. No person can take any of that from you, unless you allow them. Don't allow them to steal your joy."

Lifting my visor, I took another deep breath, then started my car and backed out the driveway to go home. As I drove, I planned my evening down to the minute. The first things on the agenda were to run a hot bath, pour a glass of wine and walk around butt-ass naked. After soaking in the hot water for at least twenty minutes, I planned to eat dinner, then read until I got sleepy.

Once I'd gotten inside and sat my bag down on the countertop, my phone started to ring. I dug through my purse for it, to see my mother was calling me. "Yes, mom?"

"I really am sorry."

"I know. I have to go, though. I'll call you tomorrow," I said as I pulled the bottle of wine from the fridge.

"Okay."

I ended the call, still hot around the collar. The anger I felt toward myself was what was eating me alive. I allowed her to take me there. The urge to curse her out was so strong, it scared me. After pouring a glass of wine, I gulped it, poured another, then went to my bedroom. I sat the glass on my dresser, then stripped down to my bra and panties and started my bath. Once I poured in some lavender, I stood in the mirror and braided my hair.

I turned on the smooth sounds of Robert Glasper and Lalah Hathaway, then sat my wine on the floor beside the tub with my phone and lowered myself slowly into the water. Exhaling all of my frustrations, I laid back on my towel pillow and closed my eyes. That didn't last long, though. My phone started ringing, interrupting my playlist. I just knew it was Mary. She never knew how to leave well enough alone. Snatching my phone from the floor, I answered, "Yeah?"

"That's how you answer the phone now?"

I sat straight up in my water. It was Zayson. "Shit. I mean... uhh... I'm sorry."

He chuckled. "What'chu so nervous for?"

"Sorry. I thought you were my mom. She irritated me to no end, so I came home."

"How did she irritate you?"

"Well... what she did didn't irritate me half as bad as I irritated myself. I wasn't prepared for her shenanigans, today. I allowed her to steal my joy from me by hurting my feelings."

"Oh. Well, hopefully you're feeling better about things now."

"I am. I'm soaking in my tub."

"Mmm."

"What?"

"Nothing. I just wanted to check on you. I'm just leaving my parents' house. I have to go shower and eat, then, if it isn't too late, I'll call back. I just didn't want to risk not hearing your voice again, tonight."

I smiled and allowed my body to relax again. The way he made me feel was insane. "Well, I'm glad you called."

"Me, too. Hopefully, I can call back, but if not, I'll see you Sunday, about ten-thirty?"

"Yes. Good night, in case it's late."

"Good night, beautiful."

And, just like that, the feelings swirling inside of me, about what happened today with Mary Hebert, were long gone because all I could think about was Zayson Ardoin.

As I drove west, on Highway 90, I could feel my nerves trying to get the best of me. What would his parents think of me? It was so soon to be meeting parents. I had no intentions of letting him meet my mother any time soon. She could be so judgmental, sometimes, and I wasn't prepared to be embarrassed by her behavior. Following the turn-by-turn directions to Zayson's house, I looked at the time to see I was early. It was only ten.

The navigation was saying I was only five minutes from his house and, the closer I got, the more nervous I became. Taking deep breaths, I turned up Le'Andrea Johnson's "Better Days." I didn't know why I was listening to this song, because it always made me cry. The lyrics touched close to home. By the time the song went off, I was in

Zayson's driveway. He had a nice one-level, log cabin-looking home, with a porch that wrapped around the house. It was beyond nice. It was gorgeous. I noticed the barn to the right of it and the horses in the pasture.

I got out of the car, slowly, while looking around. Zayson had a lot of property. Walking to the front door, I looked at the rocking chairs on the porch and smiled, as I imagined his mom and dad sitting there when they visited. Finally, I rang the doorbell as the breeze blew through my natural curls, putting my mind at ease. As I looked around once again, I heard the door opening. My lips parted as I looked at Zayson from head to toe. He wore black slacks and a wife beater, with some nice, square-toed black shoes. "You're early. Come on in."

I smiled at him, then walked inside, as his eyes seemed to follow my every movement. Once he closed the door, he said, "You look amazing, Kortlynn. I almost cussed. I gotta keep my mind right before going to church. I'll tell you what I really thought once we get out."

I giggled. "Thank you. You look great, too."

Suddenly, the smell of something delicious filled my nose. I adjusted my rose-pink dress as he continued to stare at me. "Thank you. Follow me to the kitchen. I made us French toast, eggs and bacon. The church is only right down the street, so we have plenty of time."

"You cook, too?"

"Girl, I'm a master, at this stove, when it comes to breakfast. I can barbeque, too, but that's about it."

"Well, I'm sure your mom helps with the rest, huh?"

"Yep. She cooks most of the time for me."

"Just spoiled."

"Nope, not spoiled. I do things for them and she does things for me. Hopefully, she doesn't embarrass me today. She can be loud and tacky sometimes, but she's friendly."

He pulled out a bar stool for me and I sat and looked around his home. It was beautiful and immaculate. My nose brought my attention back to the plate Zayson sat in front of me. "This looks amazing, Zayson."

"Thank you, baby girl."

"This house is beautiful, too. It's not the bachelor pad I was expecting."

"Girl, I'm thirty-four years old. I'm on my grown man shh..." He laughed. "See you almost made me cuss before church. I'm about to put some food in my mouth."

I laughed, then grabbed his hand. He stared at me until I bowed my head and said grace. When I finished, he grabbed the French toast from his plate and held it to my mouth. I took a bite and it was so good. Putting my hand over my mouth, I said, "Wow. This is really good!"

He smiled and began eating his food, as I indulged in mine, being sure not to waste anything on my light-colored dress. By the time we were done, it was ten-thirty, so Zayson went to finish getting dressed. I stood from my seat and brought our plates to the sink. Had I not been dressed to impress, I would have cleaned his kitchen for him. I walked around, looking at pictures of who I took to be his parents. When Zayson rejoined me, he had on a white long-sleeved shirt with a diagonally striped, yellow, white and black tie. He coordinated with my yellow earrings and shoes and it made me smile. "Wow. You clean up nice."

Without responding, he walked closer to me and pulled me in his arms. "Sorry, I didn't hug you earlier."

Being careful not to touch his clothes with my cheek, I pulled away and looked at him. "Quit looking at me like that. You making me wanna just stay here."

My eyebrows lifted. Stay here and do what exactly? He couldn't have thought that sex would pop off that easily. Just because I was feeling him and everything about him, didn't mean he would be feeling my insides this soon. He grabbed my hand and led me outside. "Since you so dressed up, you wanna go in your car?"

"Yeah, please. I can't have any mishaps like last time."

He chuckled, then opened the driver's door of my Mercedes. After he got in, almost hitting his head, he stared at me. "Looks like we just have issues with each other's vehicles. I almost knocked myself out just now."

I laughed, then started the car and headed to the church that I passed up on the way here, about two miles down the road.

Chapter Six

Z ayson

"HEY, HONEY. YOU'RE GORGEOUS."

"Thank you, Mrs. Ardoin."

"You're welcome. Did you enjoy the service?" my mama said while winking at me.

I rolled my eyes, then leaned against the counter. "Yes, ma'am, I did. Is there something I can do to help?"

My mama's eyebrows shot up and she gave me an under-eyed look. "I don't need any help, baby. I'm just warming the food. Everything's cooked already. Zayson is always sure to get here just in time to eat. He miscalculated this time by about ten minutes."

Kortlynn laughed at my mama, then they really started talking. "I'm going meet Daddy. Behave, Barbara."

"Behave? Boy, get'cho ass out my kitchen."

I shook my head, as I twisted my lips sideways. It probably wasn't a good decision to leave Kortlynn alone with the instigator, but I couldn't bear the sly looks she was giving me. Not long after I left, I could hear them laughing. As long as Kortlynn was enjoying herself, I guess I'd handle the embarrassment of it all later. After sitting on the couch, near my daddy, Kortlynn laughed loudly, making me wanna go back in that kitchen. "It's too late, na. I'm sure yo' mama done said something off the wall crazy about you."

He chuckled and I couldn't help but roll my eyes. "She's a nice young woman, son. You did good."

"She is nice. I wish I could have gotten to know her a little better before bringing her here to y'all two crazies."

"Well, how you expect us to act? We're damn near delusional seeing that you brought a woman here. Everybody got grandkids but us. As long as Kerry still acting like he ten years old, all our chips on you. Ain't no woman want no irresponsible, childish ass man."

Oh, Lawd. Here we go. I quickly cut him off, before he got cranked up about Kerry. "Well, Kortlynn and I aren't a couple. We just tryna get to know each other."

"Y'all might as well be a couple while y'all doing that. No need in wasting valuable time," my daddy said, as the hens in the kitchen burst into laughter.

"Sounds like they've made more of a connection than me and her."

Daddy rolled his eyes as Mama walked in and said, "Y'all come to the table."

When I walked in the dining area, Kortlynn was standing there with a plate in her hands. Once I sat, she placed it on the charger in front of me. Damn, it was like that? I looked up at her. "Wow. Thank you."

I wasn't expecting that from her. She was a guest. Mama sat Daddy's plate in front of him, then they went back to the kitchen and returned with drinks. They left, once again, to get their plates, then came back and sat next to us. The urge to kiss Kortlynn was really strong now. Those pink lips were screaming at me. She bowed her head and her yellow earrings swung to her face. She had a sense of style that couldn't be fucked with. She'd paired yellow earrings and yellow heels with a rose-pink dress. She was so damn sexy. When I realized she was the one blessing the food, I couldn't stop staring at her. My mama nudged me with her foot, under the table, and nodded her head, repeatedly, as Kortlynn prayed.

When she finished, I looked at her for a second. "Any woman that can claim Zay's attention with a plate of food in his face gotta be special as hell," my mama said.

I exhaled loudly as Kortlynn giggled. Grabbing her hand again, she looked at me. "Is everything okay?"

"Way more than okay."

I kissed her hand, as I could see my mama and daddy elbowing each other in my peripheral. Kortlynn blushed, then averted her gaze to her food. I released her hand and gave that roast, yams, mustard greens, rice, black-eyed peas and cornbread my undivided attention. We engaged in small talk as we ate, and baby girl held her own with my parents. It seemed like they'd known one another for a long ass time. By the time we'd eaten some banana pudding and were leaving, Kortlynn and I had gotten extremely comfortable with one another. She'd stroked my cheek, a couple of times, and I'd wrapped my arms around her waist.

After getting to my house, I turned to her. "Are you gonna come in for a little while?"

She fidgeted in her seat, for a minute, then looked in my eyes. She was so turned on, I could see that shit just from her gaze. "I probably shouldn't. It's already six and I need to get ready for my day tomorrow."

I bit my bottom lip, then decided to risk it all and kiss her beautiful lips. When I leaned in and she didn't back away, I knew I'd made the right decision. Her lips were so damn soft. I could feel my dick hardening, as I eased away from her. "I'm sorry. I've been wanting to do that shit all day."

"No apologies needed." She leaned over and gently kissed my

lips again. "I really enjoyed today. Your mom is so hilarious. I wish we would have had more time."

"It's okay. I don't plan for this to be the last time we're in one another's presence."

She blushed as I brushed my thumb over her bottom lip, then kissed her again. Quickly, I exited the car before I couldn't contain myself. "Call me when you get home."

"Okay. Bye."

"Bye. Be careful."

She nodded her head, then backed out of my driveway. I couldn't move until she was no longer in sight. We should have left my parents' house sooner, but Kortlynn and Mama were getting along so well. Just from their chatter, I'd learned so much about her. She was her mom's only child but had one sibling through her father. Not meeting her father until she was ten years old took me by surprise. I supposed growing up in a two-parent home with parents who loved the hell out of their children was a luxury a lot of people didn't have.

She'd talked a lot about her interests and her childhood, and I couldn't help but soak all that shit in like a sponge. I had a horse to start working on tomorrow but, before I began, I planned to either take her to lunch or bring her lunch. She'd expressed how much she liked combination rice and eggrolls, so I was gonna make sure she got that tomorrow, along with a bouquet of fresh tulips, her favorite flower. Barbara's big mouth was good for something. She'd practically played twenty-one questions with Kortlynn. Whenever my mama was being playful and clowning around, I referred to her as Barbara, which was most of the time. There were those rare times when she was being serious. Those were the times I called her Ma or Mama.

Before going in the house, I walked out to the pasture to see that crazy ass horse running all over the place, trying to get out of my fence. I had news for his ass tomorrow. When I got on his ass, he was gon' realize he was dealing with a real one. People brought their horses to me, because I was the fucking best, within a hundred-mile radius. I'd been known to break a wild horse in as little as two weeks. There was a lot of repetition.

No excitement was involved, like the rodeo events, but it made me a decent living. My back hit the dirt sometimes, but that was part of the job.

Training horses for rodeo events was different but the same. There was a lot of repetition that could make for a long day sometimes. However, once I got started, it was hard to stop, if shit wasn't at the stage I wanted by the end of the day. I wasn't expecting too much progress, tomorrow, since I would be getting a late start. I watched the stallion a little while longer, studying some of his mannerisms, then went inside the house. As soon as I took off my shoes, my phone started ringing. "Yeah, Ma?"

"That's your wife, boy! Is she still there?"

"No. She went home."

"She a good girl. You mess this up, I'm gon' tie yo' ass to that barbed wired fence and let those wild horses have a go at'cho ass."

"Barbara! Really?" She laughed loudly. "I realize how special she is, though. So, you ain't gotta worry about that."

"You know I was asking all those questions for your benefit. I hope yo' ass was listening."

"I waaaaas. Now, go tend to the business that pays you."

"I'm gon' beat yo' ass, Zay."

"Well, I gotta go. She's calling me now."

"Bye."

I ended the call, then went to my room. I knew that would get her ass off the phone. Kortlynn wasn't even calling me yet. Talking about Kortlynn only made me realize just how special she was. All the chicks I used to fool around with weren't nowhere near her level. That was why my parents were beyond excited to meet Kortlynn. None of the others were worth bringing to my parents' house. My mama would have torn them to shreds.

I exhaled, then laid in the bed. Taking a shower was out of the question, until she called. I needed to know that she'd made it safely. Turning on the TV, I began watching my recording of Tombstone. That was my shit. Wyatt Earp was a bad muthafucka. Just as I was getting into it, my phone started to ring. Pressing pause, I saw it was Kortlynn. "Hello?"

"Hey, Zayson. I'm home."

"Good. I enjoyed having your company today."

"I enjoyed it, too. I have a question."

"What's up?"

"Are you involved with anybody?"

"What?"

"I guess what I'm asking, is if I can post our pictures on social media. I don't want nobody coming for me."

"You mean to tell me you can't hold your own?"

"Huh?"

"Let me quit fucking wit'chu. I'm single, Kortlynn and I ain't messing with nobody. Hopefully, that won't be for long, though."

She got extremely quiet. So, I continued. "What'chu thinking? You wouldn't consider being with me?"

"Yeah, I would consider it. I'm just a little shocked that you thinking about a relationship already."

"Why not? I know what I want. I'm done playing games. Plus, everything about you is screaming at me to put you on lock."

"I just wanted to be sure. I just sent you a friend request."

I put the phone on speaker, then went to my Facebook app and accepted her friend request. Once I did, she immediately tagged me in a picture. It was a picture she took of us before we went in church. We looked so good together. "I like that picture."

"Yeah, me, too."

"What time do you have to get up?"

"I usually get up about six."

"Do you have a lunch break?"

"Yeah. I have a break at noon. I rarely leave, though."

"Well, would you be willing to leave tomorrow?"

"Yeah. Are you coming to meet me?"

"Yeah. I just have this undeniable urge to be around you all the time." I could hear her breathing and I could tell she had something to say. "Kortlynn?"

"Yes?"

"You don't ever have to be shy or afraid to express yourself. We grown ass individuals. What's on your mind?"

"I was just thinking about what you said about wanting to be with me. I want to be with you, too, Zayson. Everything about this feels so right. What I don't know about you, I can get to know. But like you said, I wanna put you on lock, too. Every woman in that diner looked at you a little too long, even while I was with you. I don't wanna see you with anyone but me."

"Well, damn. Take ownership of me, then, baby girl."

She giggled, as I thought about how much like my dad she sounded. There wasn't much for her to know about me, but I could tell she had layers and I wanted to be the nigga to expose them all.

Chapter Seven

K ortlynn

"So there's no confusion, you telling me you wanna be my woman, right?"

"Yeah. Are you telling me you wanna be my man, Roger Troutman?"

"That's exactly what I'm telling you. In a short time, I feel like I can't live my life without you."

"Look at you! Quoting song lyrics and shit!"

He laughed loudly. Today had been beyond amazing. Mrs. Barbara had told me so much about Zayson and how stubborn and hard-headed he could be, but he was showing me just the opposite. He was a sweetheart and didn't seem to have a problem expressing just how he felt. She'd also told me that he was a good man that just needed the right woman to complete him and that she could already see that woman was me. Zayson seemed to be everything I wanted in a man and I could tell he was being different with me by the looks on his parents' faces, especially when he kissed my hand. He'd done that several times and I was dying to feel his lips on mine.

When he finally gave in to it, I thought I had died and went on to Glory. Minnie Ripperton was singing "Lovin' You" and the birds were chirping in the background. I didn't want him to stop but, I knew if he didn't, I would have been going inside his house, doing all sorts of things I would regret later. God, his lips were so soft. The heat stirring between us was almost unbearable, so I was glad that he hurriedly got out of my car. He was feeling the same way I was feeling.

Zayson James Ardoin. His mama had told me his middle name was James because she had a thing for James Earl Jones, back in the day. It was one of the many moments we'd laughed loudly. "You know, your lil hood voice comes out without warning and it feels like it chokes the shit out me when I hear it 'cause I'm not expecting it."

It was my turn to laugh. I looked at the time and knew I needed to take a shower. "As much as I enjoy talking to you, I have to go take a shower and prepare for tomorrow. I'll call you back, when I get in bed."

"Aight, baby girl. I'm gonna take a shower, too, while I wait for you to call back."

"Okay."

I ended the call on cloud nine, excited as hell. Kortlynn Denise Hebert had a boyfriend for the first time in years; almost ten to be exact. Patience was definitely a virtue, because ten years was a long time to wait. I hadn't had sex in almost five years, and Zayson was making me want to end my streak today. Although, he tried to hide it, I saw his erection when he got out of the car. It was something to brag about and, when the time was right, I'd experience every inch of it.

After turning my music on, I started the shower, then just leaned against the linen closet. This man had me swooning and I just hoped I wasn't feeling this way prematurely. I was almost totally invested. While my guard was crumbling, with every word that left his lips, it was still there, bracing for disappointment. My phone chimed, breaking me from my thoughts. It was a text from Legend. *So y'all were discussing gardening at Mrs. Barbara and Mr. Henry's house?*

I knew his ass was trying to be funny. I sent back laughing emojis, then responded. *Why didn't you tell me how fine he was and that I wouldn't be able to resist his charm?*

He quickly sent back the sick emojis and one throwing up. I laughed, loudly, like he was standing next to me. He'd seen my pictures on Facebook. I'd posted a picture of us in front of the church and another at his parents' house. I sat my phone back on the countertop and let Rachelle Ferrell's voice further relax me, as I put on my shower cap and got in the shower.

Zayson seemed to like my hair in its natural curly state. When we'd sat on the couch, he'd twirled a strand of it with his fingers. It was one of those moments his parents had looked shocked. Looking in his eyes, as he did so, was too much for me. The desire to feel him in every way imaginable had invaded my thoughts and that was so inappropriate in front of his parents. It took me a minute to even rejoin the conversation after that. I was so caught up in his admiration, that I could barely focus on anything else.

My shower lasted a little longer than normal because thoughts of Zayson gave me pause. It was like he'd taken over my ability to function and it made me feel amazing. Knowing that there was a man in my life that had the power to control my thoughts was refreshing. I wasn't desperate for a man. Otherwise, I wouldn't have gone the past ten years without one or the past five years without sex. I'd reached a point in my life where I was enough for me. So, for him to come in like a whirlwind and sweep me off my feet said a lot.

When I crawled in bed, it was nearly nine and the yawn that overtook me let me know how long the day had been. Grabbing my phone, I went to my recent calls to call Zay... my boyfriend. Just that thought had me giddy like a schoolgirl. His phone rang a few times, then went to voicemail. My lip poked out and I ended the call without leaving a message, hoping I hadn't taken too long to call. I laid there, on my back, trying to stay awake, hoping he'd call me back.

My phone chimed, alerting me of a text and I jumped out my skin. It was my cousin, J'Neka, in Denton. I was so hoping that it was Zayson. It read, *Who in the hell is that?*

I chuckled. I hadn't talked to her this past week, so I knew she would want the juice. *My new boyfriend.*

I smiled when I sent the message. She was gon' want all the details. Before her response could come through, Zayson called back. "Hello?"

"Hey, baby girl. Sorry, but your cousin and his wing man were on my ass. Threatening to kill me and shit if I hurt you." He chuckled, then asked in serious tone, "You know I would never hurt you intentionally, right?"

"I feel that about you. I'm already anticipating tomorrow."

"Shiiiid, me, too. I can't wait until we've gotten to the level where we're even more comfortable around each other."

I got quiet, because I needed him to clarify. Was he talking about sex? I knew he was a sexual being, but he said he'd been doing without it for the past few months. "Say what you mean, Zayson."

Listening to him breathe was doing shit to me and I knew there would be nights that I'd have to please myself. We'd had our first real kiss today and he had my hormones in overdrive. "I wish you could have stayed with me. I wanna just hold you in my arms, play in your hair and kiss your beautiful lips."

I closed my eyes, as he spoke, imagining everything he was saying. Zayson was saying he wanted to show me intimacy. If I could handle that without wanting more was the question. His words had my middle feeling extra sensitive and I knew that if his words could do that, then his touch and his kiss would take me out. When I experienced all of him, I wanted to be in love with him. If I could hold out until then, I would be amazed with myself, though. "Kortlynn. Say something, baby."

That deep, raspy voice was about to kill me. Slowly exhaling, I began, "I can't wait until we're at that level either. I just want us to both be ready before we go there."

"I know. Your kiss was amazing today. I can't stop thinking about it."

"Me either."

"Well, I should probably let you go to sleep, since you have to get up early."

"What if I don't want to hang up?"

"You ain't said shit. I'll sit on this phone with you all night."

I giggled. Falling for him would be easy. From the first phone conversation, he'd had my attention. "I wish I could talk to you all night, but you're right. I'm not going to want to get up in the morning. I can't wait to see you tomorrow."

"I can't wait to see you either. Sleep well, beautiful."

"Good night, Zayson."

⚘

I TOSSED AND TURNED ALL NIGHT, UNTIL I GOT MY DILDO AND stroked myself to sleep. I had to dust the damn thing off. It had to have been at least a year since I'd last used it. But Zayson's words wouldn't let me go. The sensuality in them was too much. Sitting at my desk, it seemed I couldn't read a thing without losing focus. That was until there was a knock on my door. It was only eleven, so it couldn't have been Zayson already. Going to the door, I opened it to see Ms. Taylor. She smiled brightly and she had someone with her. It was a beautiful, chocolate goddess. Ms. Taylor looked great; a lot better than she did the last time I saw her.

She seemed to look about the same as she did before she went missing. I smiled brightly and stepped aside to let them enter my office. "Hello, Ms. Taylor! It's so good to see you."

"Hi, Kortlynn! I told you to call me Serita. This is my sister, Sidney. She's the attorney for Integrity. She's also the wife of Devin Taylor, the accountant you've been working with."

"Wow. It's nice to meet you Attorney Taylor. You represented my cousin, a year or two ago. Legend Semien."

"Yes! The bull rider. It's nice to meet you, Kortlynn. Call me Sidney."

They sat in the chairs in front of my desk and I straightened the paperwork I had scattered there, then sat as well. I was hoping that this was a friendly visit and that I hadn't done anything to warrant this trip. Serita sat back in her chair as Sidney flipped her long ponytail over her shoulder. I could clearly see that it was her natural hair. "Kortlynn, I just want you to know that you are doing an amazing job. I know I left things in a mess and you had so much to figure out. I appreciate you for making sure the business side of things was handled first. Without those funds, it would be impossible to keep the center running."

I was waiting on the 'but' and what she had to say after, so I felt like I was still holding my breath. She giggled. "Relax. I wanted to tell you that I wanted to come back and volunteer my time, helping with the girls and programs."

I finally released the breath I was holding as Sidney laughed. "I would love to have you back. I bring your name up in every staff meeting and reiterate your vision for the program. My boyfriend is going to come at the end of next month to teach the girls gardening. He's a farmer."

"Oh, that's great! Do you farm with him?"

I lowered my head, then looked up at them. "No. He became my boyfriend after I met with him about teaching the girls."

We all broke out in laughter, as someone knocked at my door. Looking at the time, I saw it was eleven thirty. That was probably Zayson. "Looks like you may get to meet him, because he's bringing me to lunch today."

"Oooh. Sidney, we were right on time," Serita said, then giggled as they stood.

When I opened the door, Zay was standing there with a bouquet of orange, yellow and pink tulips. He wore the biggest smile and I couldn't help but smile back. Once he walked inside, he stopped. "I'm sorry, baby girl. I didn't mean to interrupt your meeting."

"Oh, no. This is just a casual visit," Serita said.

"Zayson, this is the founder of Integrity, Serita Taylor and her sister, Sidney Taylor."

He handed me the flowers and kissed my cheek, then shook Serita's outstretched hand. Him greeting me first didn't go unnoticed. Although I'd introduced him to Serita already, he was sure to acknowledge me. That shit had me proud as hell to have him as mine. "Hello, Ms. Taylor and... Ms. Taylor."

They giggled and Sidney blushed, as he shook her hand. That was cute. Zayson had that effect on every woman he came in contact with. "Hello, Zayson. Serita and Sidney," Serita said. "We're gonna get out of your way. Kortlynn, I'll see you probably Wednesday, if that's okay for me to start."

"That's perfect. We have a meeting Thursday. Everyone will be glad to see you."

I hugged her and Sidney, then they giggled as they left. Zayson pulled me in his arms. "What's so funny? If I didn't know any better, I'd think y'all were talking about me."

"We were. I'd just told them that you became my boyfriend after meeting about the gardening program."

"Ahh. No wonder. How did you sleep? Did you get my text?"

"I slept well when I finally fell asleep. Sorry, I hadn't checked my phone. It's in my purse and it's on vibrate. I'll have to get used to sitting it on my desk."

"Mmm hmm," he said, then lowered his lips to mine for a peck. "You ready to go?"

"Mmm. Your lips." I exhaled loudly, then shook my head slowly. "Let me get my purse."

"What about my lips?" he asked, then bit his bottom one.

"They feel amazing."

When I got back to him, he pulled me to him again and claimed my mouth with his. My eyes closed and I tried to concentrate on anything but the gushiness between my legs. His hands gripped me tightly, but I had to cut this kiss short. I was at work. "Sorry, Zayson."

"Naw, it's my bad. It's just hard controlling myself around you."

"Shit, you have no idea."

We left and he refused to tell me where we were going. The ride was quiet, as I sat anticipating. When he pulled into Taste of China's parking lot, I started dancing in my seat as he laughed. I loved combination rice, especially from here. Their shrimp were so huge. "You love Chinese food that much?"

"Yes! What's your favorite food?"

"Anything barbequed."

"You ever danced because you were excited to get it?"

"Naw."

"Liar."

We laughed, as he got out the truck to open my door. I was extra careful, especially since I'd worn a floor-length dress. As I stepped out onto the running board, Zayson picked me up and sat me on the cement. I stared up at him. "Thank you."

"I didn't want you to get distracted."

I giggled. "Stop!"

Once we'd gone inside and ordered our food, I couldn't help but sit at the table and stare at him. He seemed to be getting a little uneasy, so I said, "I was really impressed today."

"Why? Cause I paid attention to y'all game of twenty-one questions?"

I frowned to signal my confusion, then quickly realized he was talking about me and his mama yesterday. I giggled then said, "No, silly. The way you greeted me first, even after I'd introduced you to Serita and Sidney."

"Was that a test?"

"No, but I noticed. Thank you."

"Ain't nobody more important than you. You don't have to thank me. You should expect it... hell, demand it."

"We're still new. I don't want you to think I'm nagging or complaining."

"How else will I know, sweetheart?" he asked, then tapped my nose.

I smiled at him, then shuddered from the chill that went up my spine just from his touch. There was no way I was gonna get any work done when I got back to the office. "So, why was the founder there today?" he asked breaking me from my thoughts.

"She said she wanted to say thank you for keeping everything up and that she wanted to start volunteering."

Zayson frowned. It was like his wheels started turning. "What is it?"

"If she's the founder, why would she be coming back to volunteer? That sounds weird to me."

"She had a drug problem and had to get herself together. I think she just wants to get out of the house."

"How's she paying her bills?"

"Her ex-husband is a billionaire. And her sister that was with her is a millionaire. The entire family is well off."

"You don't think she wants the center back?"

"I hope not. I did beg her to keep it open. She was going to close it until she was ready to come back to it. Shit. I might lose my job."

"Kortlynn, don't panic. I just don't want you to be shocked if that is what happens. You need to be prepared, just in case."

He grabbed my hands as my appetite left me. Just the smell of the food was making me sick to my stomach. Serita wouldn't do that to me. Would she? My mind was going crazy from the possibilities. Even if she wanted it back, she wouldn't fire me. She would definitely demote me, though. The cashier brought our food to the table. Since people rarely sat inside to eat, they didn't have wait staff. I looked up at Zayson to see the worry on his face. I started to pick over my food, but I couldn't even force the fork to my mouth. "I'm sorry. I ruined our lunch, huh?"

I lifted my hand to his cheek and stroked it. He grabbed my hand

and held it in between his and kissed it. "Lunch isn't ruined. I'm just worried."

"Let's box this up. I wanna take you somewhere. Is it okay if you're a little late getting back?"

"Yeah, as long as I'm not too late."

"Aight."

Once Zayson got our boxes and boxed up our food, he helped me in his truck and brought me to Mane Event Spa. "I'm gonna get you a relaxation massage, and I'll be back in thirty minutes to pick you up. I wanted to get you an hour, but I know you don't have time."

I couldn't take advantage of him this way. "Zayson, this is so sweet. But I know you have business to handle. I'll be fine. I promise."

He lowered his head, but I was grateful that he made me see the more commonsense side of what was probably happening. Serita had gotten her life together and she wanted her life back; a piece of it at least. Her kids were no longer in her life, except the youngest. But the three she'd had with her ex-husband, Shawn Taylor, were now living with him. I lifted Zayson's head and kissed his lips. "This is all I need to make me feel better."

He gave me a smirk. "Well, in that case, bring them lips back to ya man."

And that I did, until it felt like we were getting carried away. I was grateful for his tinted windows. Zayson had begun caressing my back and making his way to my ass. When I pulled away from him, I giggled at the burgundy lipstick all over his lips. Grabbing a napkin from my to-go bag, I wiped his face, as he stared at me like he was ready to dive in again. This celibacy wasn't going to last much longer.

Chapter Eight

Z ayson

I FELT LIKE SHIT FOR RUINING BABY GIRL'S MOOD, BUT I NEEDED
her to see the shit that Serita was about to do. I felt like she was
coming back as a volunteer to put Kortlynn at ease, making her think
everything was okay. Then, soon as she got back in the swing of
things, she was gonna take it back over. It was her vision, so Kortlynn
couldn't be mad if that was what she chose to do, but she could at
least be upfront about it. The fact that she didn't ask Kortlynn to do it
was the only thing that saved her ass. Had she asked Kortlynn to do it,
then that would have been something different.

I felt for my baby, though. She said she was okay, but when I
dropped her off, I could see her shoulders slump. I knew something
would happen where I didn't wanna leave her. When I woke up, at
five this morning, that feeling hit me in my gut. I was an early riser,
but never that early. I'd gotten up, put a halter on that colt and

worked his ass over real good, loping him in circles, until about ten. Loping is one of the basic steps, when it comes to breaking horses. I'd been feeding him, letting him get comfortable with me for the past week. That was so I wouldn't have too much of a problem getting him to come close to me, so I could get the halter on him.

After taking a shower, I'd come to Beaumont. I was gonna go home and get a couple more hours in, then I was gonna come back for baby girl. Grabbing my phone, I called Kortlynn. "Hello?"

"Baby, pick your head up. Okay? Ya man fucked up. I should've never said that. What time you getting off?"

"You didn't mess up. I needed to be prepared, if that happens. I'm leaving at five."

"I'm coming back to you, and I ain't taking no for an answer. You prolly don't wanna be alone with me, but I promise, we won't do anything you don't wanna do. I just need to be able to hold you. Let me do that."

She was completely quiet. I wanted her to trust me enough to be vulnerable in front of me. Although it was still soon, I knew that she was gon' be it for me, just like my parents knew. That shit was clear as day, to me, the moment I laid eyes on her. But now it was imperative that she saw that shit, too. I needed her to know that I was the only nigga for her, and I wasn't sure that she saw that as plainly as I did. "Okay. Whenever you get here, I'll be ready."

"Aight, baby. Try to make the best out of the rest of your day. When I get there, I'll take over that job for you."

"Thank you, Zayson."

"Aight. See you later."

The way she sounded was killing me and made me wanna tell this horse to go fuck himself. I couldn't wait to hold her in my arms and assure her that everything would be okay, no matter what happened. My daddy taught me how to provide for my woman and how to be there for her and whatever she needed from me. Kortlynn was the first woman I'd met that was worthy of those lessons. I knew she was independent and cared about her career but, with me, she would always have options.

When I got home, I did some quick work with the colt. He was quicker than what the owner gave him credit for. He was dropping his head like he was supposed to and stepping out with the right leg, at certain times. After working with him, for two hours, and feeding all the other horses, it was nearly four. I went inside and took a shower to make sure I didn't smell like horse shit, then made my way back to Beaumont.

I got to the center, close to five, and baby girl was sitting in her car. She looked over at me and smiled weakly, then backed up so I could follow her home. As I did, my phone rang. I rolled my eyes when I saw my brother's number, then answered. "What's up, Kerry?"

"Not too much, lil bruh. What'chu up to? I was 'bout to come out there."

"I'm not home. I'm in Beaumont."

"Oh. Oh, well."

"You need to go talk to Mama and Daddy, so they can quit hounding me."

"Aww, man. I'ma go over there. They pissed 'cause I bought this horse, but I couldn't pass up this deal. This horse is predicted to win it all."

"Then, why did the owner sell it?"

"He couldn't afford the upkeep. The guy I partnered with to get it is handling all the training and everything. I just put the money up."

"If you say so. Just talk to them and quit avoiding them. Maybe y'all can come to an understanding."

"What is there to understand? It was my money."

"Not if you owed them money, Kerry. Why wouldn't you take care of them before putting everything on the line like that?"

"You sounding like Mama. I'ma either go over there, or call them, tomorrow, when I get off."

"Aight, man."

The older that nigga got, the stupider he got. He was like a kid, thinking everybody his fucking friend. I have a feeling he 'bout to get fucked over and gon' find a way to blame everybody but himself. We turned into Kortlynn's complex and I realized she only lived five minutes from the center. They were nice apartments, from what I could tell. She pointed to the parking spots I should park in, then went to her garage. Hopping out the truck, in my wife beater, basketball shorts and slides, I walked to her garage. I wanted to be comfortable, if I was gonna be lying down to hold her.

When she got out of her car, her eyes swept over me and her breathing pattern changed. She wanted me, but she still had her guard up. That was evident, whenever we were around each other. I walked closer to her and pulled her in my arms. When I heard her exhale, I wanted to pick her up and carry her in the house. Her heart was heavy. "Lay that shit on me, baby. Let me carry that weight for you."

She smiled softly, then grabbed my hand and led me inside. Her place was nice. "Make yourself at home, Zayson. I'm gonna go take a shower," she said as her phone rang.

She looked at it and rolled her eyes, but still answered. "Hey, Mom. I just got home... Let me call you back... I'm okay. I'll call you back.... Mom..."

She walked away while she talked, and I sat on her couch and turned on the TV. I found a basketball game on ESPN and watched that while she handled her business. I was tired as fuck. Fooling around with that horse and in that heat had taken its toll on me. While it wasn't hard work, it was repetitive work that could wear anybody's ass out. Thirty minutes had gone by and, just as I was about to go traipsing through the kitchen, Kortlynn came walking down the hall in a long, cotton night gown. Her hair was wrapped and her face was bare of makeup. She was so damn beautiful.

I stood from my seat on the couch. "I didn't think to bring anything to eat. You hungry?"

"I still have my lunch from earlier. I ate a little bit out of it at work, but I couldn't eat it all. You want some? There's still more than what I'm gonna eat in there."

"Yeah. I didn't even think about getting something to eat. I just wanted to get to you."

She smiled, then went to the kitchen to warm the food. I followed her and slid my arms around her from behind. Kortlynn rested her head against me and I leaned over to kiss her cheek. "You're so beautiful."

"Thank you, Zayson. You're a handsome man. Aaannnd... you're all mine."

"That's right, baby. All yours."

She took the food from the microwave, then got two bowls from the cupboard, as I sat at her table. "So, how did the training go?"

"As expected. I still have plenty work to do, but I can only do so much a day."

"Maybe, one day, I can come watch."

"I promise, you don't wanna do that. You'll be bored out of your mind. Today, we walked in circles for hours."

"Okay. Maybe I'll watch a little while, then go in your house and cook."

"Now that sounds like a plan."

She smiled as she sat the bowl in front of me, then sat next to me with two bottles of water. Scooping a spoonful of rice, I held it up to her mouth. When those lips parted, and her mouth opened, I couldn't help but bite my bottom lip, as she stared at me. It seemed like everything she did, turned me on sexually. I had to ask God to forgive me, yesterday, because I'd gotten turned on while she was saying grace. Putting the spoon back in the bowl, I remembered that we hadn't said grace. "I'm sorry. We forgot to bless the food."

Putting my hand on the table, palm up, she placed her hand in mine and bowed her head. I said the grace and I could feel her eyes on me. Once I was done, she smiled and I continued feeding her and she fed me. It was so sensual, she probably wouldn't want me anywhere near her when she laid down. There was no way I could lay with her without getting hard. No way in hell.

After we finished eating, I helped her clean the mess, then we went to the couch. Pulling her closer, I draped my arm over her shoulder and handed her the remote, as she tucked her feet under herself. "We can watch the game. I like basketball."

"Well, damn. I swear you my dream girl."

She giggled then laid her head against me. Moving my arm to rest on her hip, I leaned to the arm of the sofa so she could get more comfortable. "This feels nice, Zay."

"Beyond nice."

This position was safe, although, I still wanted to grab her ass. That shit was just sitting up, staring at me, like, *squeeze me, Zay.* Somehow, I was able to resist the urge. We laid there, quietly watching the game, or so I thought. I looked down to see baby girl had gone straight to sleep. Gently shaking her, I awoke her from her slumber. "Let's go to bed."

Her eyebrows shot up. "Zay, you can't stay the night."

"Why not? I told you I just wanted to hold you. That's it."

"I'm just not comfortable with that."

I nodded. A nigga rushed and drove all the way to Beaumont to sit here for two hours. Helping her to her feet, after I stood, I was about to lead her to her bedroom, but she led me to the door. "Damn, baby girl. What's up, for real?"

"Zay, we've only been together for two days. I can't do this with you yet."

"Aight. Well, I'll talk to you tomorrow, I guess."

"Call me when you get home."

I kissed her forehead and left her standing there, watching me. I thought she knew I would be staying with her. Maybe she did and knew I would still come anyway. I wanted to be frustrated, but my heart wouldn't let me be. She was right. We'd only been together two days and known each other for four. I was tripping. Taking a deep breath, I got in my truck and headed home. As I got on Highway 90, my phone was ringing. It was Kortlynn. Why was she calling already? "Hello?"

"I'm sorry, Zay."

"You don't owe me an apology. You're right. I'm tryna move too fast. It's just that I know that you the only one for me and I know I'm the only nigga for you. Real shit. But I'm gonna be patient, until you can see that shit for yourself."

She was quiet, so we just sat on the phone, listening to each other breathe, my whole way to China.

Chapter Nine

K ortlynn

My nerves were on edge. I thought Zayson was gonna be mad at me for making him leave. I didn't know he was planning to spend the night with me. I thought he would just stay until I went to bed. I'd called to apologize and he was so understanding. We literally listened to each other breathe, for almost fifteen minutes, on the phone until he'd made it home. He bid me good night, and I laid in the bed, in my feelings, until I fell asleep an hour later.

It had been a week since that night, and Zayson and I had been talking every day, but I went almost the whole week without seeing him. I knew he was trying to give me space, until I got to know him, but I missed him. Yesterday, I couldn't take it anymore and showed up at his house, to find him outside without a shirt on. That tatted chest was everything. I sat in the car, for at least five minutes, watching him. We'd sat on his porch and talked for about an hour, then he went back to what he was doing.

Today, he was supposed to be coming to the center to plant a test crop. Serita had come last week and it was great having her around. I was panicking, last week, but I knew I would always have a place here. I was beyond passionate about this place. Even if she took it back over, I probably wouldn't leave. That was how much I believed in her cause: educating these girls and letting them see the wealth of opportunities available to them.

There was a knock on my doorframe, so I looked up to see Zayson. "Hey, Kortlynn. I just wanted to let you know I was here. I'm gonna head outside."

"Hey. Can we talk when you're done?"

"Yeah. Of course."

He walked away and I watched him go outside. I hated this distant Zayson. It was my fault, but he was just wanting to take things too fast. What I didn't expect was for him to pull all the way back, like we had never been intimate. I exhaled hard, then lowered my face to my hands. "You okay?"

Looking up, I saw Serita standing at the door with a cup of coffee. "I'm okay. I'm just having doubts about Zayson. Well... not doubts. It's just that he's wanting to move a lot faster and I had to pump his brakes. Now, he's being distant with me. In the past week, besides today, we only saw each other once."

"Well, he probably feels like that's the only way he can control himself. You're a beautiful woman, Kortlynn."

"Thank you, Serita. Maybe so. I asked him to come talk to me when he was done."

"What's he doing?"

"Planting a test crop, to see how it does. He said he didn't want the girls to feel like they failed, if nothing popped up out the ground."

"Hmm. Smart." Serita looked nervous for a moment. "Can I ask you something?"

"Sure."

I didn't feel good about this. It felt like she was gonna say something to hurt me. She wasn't really the type to intentionally hurt anyone except her sister, Sonya. I'd witness their exchanges. They were anything but nice. "If I wanted to take full control of Integrity, would that hurt you?"

Zayson was right. Staring in her eyes, I asked, "Would I still have a job?"

"Of course! Your pay would stay the same and you would be the assistant director. You would still be doing most of what you're doing now. The only thing is that we would talk about programs to implement before we brought it to the rest of the staff."

"That wouldn't hurt me at all, Serita. Thank you."

She walked over to me and hugged me tightly. "I have something for you. Shawn, my ex-husband, was gracious enough to bless me with some money, so I want to give you this."

She handed me an envelope that I hadn't even noticed she'd been holding. I was so nervous about what she had to say, she could've been holding a damn snake and it wouldn't have caught my attention. Hesitantly, I opened the envelope to see a cashier's check for ten thousand dollars. "Serita! What is this for?!"

The tears fell from her eyes. "You did me a favor... a huge one. Even though I didn't ask you to. Had I closed the center, it would have been extremely hard to get my government funding back. This program means so much to me. But I let stupid decisions threaten everything I built. I'm sure you know, but I allowed Cooper's dad to persuade me to use cocaine. Every time I think about it, I realize just how blessed I am to still be alive. My family saved my children. I could have lost them and this center. But God had other plans. I owe you so much more and, when I can afford to, I will compensate you."

I hugged her tightly and, at that moment, I felt sorry for her. She gently pulled away from me and wiped her face. "Now... You quit being so scared of falling for that man out there. Just judging from the first time I met him, this has to be killing him more than it's killing you. The way he looked at you reminded me of how Shawn used to look at me. I destroyed our relationship... our family. Don't let your fears and your past experiences alter your future. Every day, I wish I could take back what I did to him... how I crushed him. But now it's too late. Don't procrastinate, Kortlynn. Go to him, now."

I hesitantly walked out of my office, fear of what he would say practically crippling me. When I got to the door, I saw him on his knees in the dirt. Taking a deep breath, I opened the door and saw the sweat dripping down his face and arms. He stood, then took off his shades and stared at me. "Hey. You need something?"

I nodded my head, as I let the door close behind me. "Okay. Let me water this and I'll be done. When I do this for the girls, I'll bring a tiller and my other gardening tools."

He took a moment to water what he'd planted, then wrapped the hose and sat it against the building. Looking at the time, I noticed it was practically my lunch hour. *Time to quit playing it safe, Kort. All or nothing.* When he walked over to me, he used the towel on his shoulder to wipe his face. "What's up, baby girl?"

"Did you bring any clothes to change into?"

"Naw. After this, I'm going home and try to get on this colt. Hopefully, he don't buck my ass off. He just got used to having the saddle on him."

"Can I come?"

"Nobody else will be there, baby." He exhaled hard. "I'm trying to respect your wishes, but this shit is hard. I just wanna..."

I didn't let him finish. I pulled his face to mine and kissed him like my life depended on it. He needed to know that I wanted him. That week, barely talking to him, was so hard for me. Zayson pulled away from me. "What are you saying to me, Kortlynn?"

"I miss you. I'm willing to stop living in fear of what might happen and just go with the flow. You respect me so much, but last week was so hard. Not seeing you or talking to you as much, hurt my heart."

"I will never disrespect you. I'm so glad you understand how much you mean to me already."

"Let me get my things."

"Okay."

My heart was beating rapidly, as he walked along the side of the building to his truck. Going back in the cool air, I exhaled loudly, then closed my eyes for a moment. That wasn't as hard as I thought it would be. "I assumed it worked out?"

I opened my eyes to see Serita. "Yes. Thank you for the encouragement. There's more that I want to talk to him about, but we're moving in the right direction. Can I take the rest of the day off?"

She smiled. "Why are you asking me? You're still the director."

I smiled back, then went to the office and grabbed my bag, along with a change of clothes. When I got outside, Zayson's truck was gone. My heart sank a little as my phone rang. Pulling it from my bag, I saw it was Zay. "Hello?"

"Hey, baby. I left to get home and take a shower before you got here."

"Okay. You want something to eat?"

"Yeah, please? Whatever you get is cool."

"Okay. I'll be there in about thirty to forty-five minutes."

"Aight, baby."

I ended the call and got in my car. The happiness in his tone made *me* happy and I couldn't wait to see where my admission would lead us. After getting us some Mexican food from Carmelo's and I made the drive to China, my phone rang. Seeing it was mother, I answered through the Bluetooth. "Hello?"

"Hi, Kortlynn. Are you at lunch?"

"Hi, mom. No. I'm on my way to meet my boyfriend."

"Boyfriend? Why am I just hearing about this?"

"I wanted to make sure that I wanted to be with him, without restraint, first."

"What do you mean without restraint?"

I rolled my eyes slightly. Her mind had gone to the gutter. "I meant without keeping a wall up. I'm ready to acknowledge my feelings for him and trust that he cares for me as much as I do him."

"So, when will I get to meet him?"

"Maybe this weekend. I'll have to check with him, first."

"Okay. Well, I'm happy that you're happy."

"Me, too. It's been a long time coming."

"Have you thought anymore about what we talked about?"

She was referring to the conversation she incited, against my will, when Zayson was at my place last week. "Mom, I just told you I have a boyfriend. Why would I want to go out with that trainer?"

"Well, a boyfriend isn't a husband. You should have options."

I rolled my eyes. It was like her morals were non-existent when it came to men. She and I were really nothing alike but, she seemed to think that, if my frame was smaller, I would have been more sexually experienced. "Well, I'm not trying to have my options open. I'm thirty-two years old. I'm ready to find the one and settle down. That's it."

"Okay, Kortlynn. But if he hurts you, you know I'll be the first to say I told you so. Men are cruel and heartless. Your dad left me without a look back. Sure, he came to be in your life, but after ten years! I don't want that for you."

I didn't talk much about Calvin Wyatt. I respected him for owning up to his responsibilities, but by the time he came along, it was practically too late. My mom had raised me to practically hate a man that I didn't know. So, when he came along, I was so shut off, emotionally, it took a long time for me to bond with him. We still weren't as close as I would have liked. After so long, my dad stopped coming around as much. He felt like there was no hope and that I would never love him. So, when my mama had my own personal house phone installed, I started calling him more. "Mom, I'm a grown woman. I know how to handle my affairs. I'm not that fat, little girl that cried because she didn't have any friends anymore. When are you going to realize that?"

She was quiet. It was then that I realized I not only insulted myself to make other people comfortable, I did it for my mother, too. She was the main person I did it for. Mary was quick to call me fat or tell me I would be a great catch, if I would lose weight. So, she taught me to have style, because there was nothing worse than a fat woman that didn't know how to flatter her curves. "Fine, Kortlynn Denise. I'll talk to you later."

When she didn't have a comeback, she'd hang up. She'd never admit to being wrong or that I was right. Every now and then, I got an apology when she "thought" she'd offended me. That's how she would always say it, like it wasn't done intentionally. "Okay, Mom."

She ended the call and I proceeded to Zayson's house, ready to forget about the turmoil that could sometimes come along with Mary Hebert. I was ready to just focus on him and how he made me feel. Whatever happened, happened.

Chapter Ten

Z ayson

As soon as I moisturized my skin and put on some drawers, the doorbell was ringing. My baby was here. When I got here, I looked over at that colt and told him go to hell. I had to make up with my baby. That week of not being around her was hell, so that colt was probably glad I was giving his ass a break today. I'd worked him a little this morning, before I went to the center, but the way baby girl kissed me had a nigga on top of the damn world. I had been trying to respect her. She was totally uncomfortable, when we were alone at her place, last week. However, I knew it would be impossible to be around her without touching her in some way. I wasn't sure what happened, but I thought she was comfortable with my touch and us being intimate.

I hurriedly put on some shorts and a t-shirt, then went to the door. Kortlynn was standing there with a gorgeous smile on her face and bags of food in her hands. I grabbed them from her, then leaned over and kissed her lips. She walked inside and closed the door behind her, as I brought the food to the kitchen. "This Mexican food? It smells good."

"Yeah. Chile con queso, Spanish rice, fajita meat, shredded cheese... you know, the works."

"I'm starving, too. I didn't eat breakfast."

I unloaded the food, then got two plates down for us, along with two bottles of water. When I sat next to her, I noticed her cleavage peeking out at me. Her burgundy dress with cream colored polka dots, stopped a little above her ankles and she wore camel colored heels. However, it was made like a wrap dress at the top. I glanced once more, then filled my plate with food while she laughed. "Yeah, you're definitely hungry. I'm glad I bought plenty."

I chuckled. "Speaking of buying, let me get you some ends for the food."

"It's my treat, Zay. I'm sorry for halting our progress. I thought I was doing what was best for me, and it turned out to be a huge mistake. God, I missed you so much."

"I missed you, too, girl."

I dropped my fork and pulled her face to mine. Kissing her slowly was turning me on and her rubbing those nails up my arm only made the moment more heated. But when she moaned in my mouth, I wanted to scoop her up and carry her to my bedroom. Slowly pulling away, I said, "Damn, that felt good." After taking a bite of my fajita, I looked over at her drizzling some queso on her nacho chips. "So, how have things been going with Serita?"

"Good. And you were right. She wants the center back. However, she wants to keep me on board, as the assistant director, letting me maintain my pay rate, and she gave me a bonus."

"Wow. That's great. If you don't mind me asking, was the bonus significant?"

"Yep. Ten grand."

I almost choked on my damn water. That was a hell of a bonus. Kortlynn laughed at me. "Damn!"

"I know! I thought the same thing. She encouraged me to go outside and talk to you right then."

"You kissed me, all sweaty and shit. You must really like my ass."

She giggled. "I really do."

We both went back to eating and I couldn't help but watch her. My mama would be so happy to know she was here. She was on my ass about making sure I didn't mess up things by moving too fast. She said a real woman wanted to be courted and that the only thing those lil girls I used to mess with wanted was sex and a good time. Hell, that was all I wanted, too. I lived in the damn country. Besides being outdoors, fooling around with the animals, the only thing to do was to have sex. There was one caution light, a post office, restaurant, two convenience stores, an elementary school, three churches and a Dollar General. That was it.

Once I ate my belly full, I cleaned the kitchen while Kortlynn went to get her bag. "Do you mind if I take a shower here?"

My eyebrows lifted. That shit was gon' drive me batshit crazy to know she was in my house, naked as the day she was born, and I couldn't see. "Why would I mind?"

She shrugged her shoulders, then came back to me in the kitchen. I leaned against the counter and she pressed her body against mine. *Aww, shit!* She was pushing her luck, for real. I grabbed her hips and pulled her closer. Leaning over, I kissed her lips, then her cheek. When she dropped her head back, I kissed her neck, then quickly pulled away. "My bad."

She looked at me, then pulled my head back to her neck. Before I could stop myself, my hands roamed to her ass. Dragging my lips across her skin, to her ear, I said in a low voice, "Maaaaaan, you better go take your shower."

"Or what?"

I pulled back to look in her eyes. She couldn't be serious right now. I swung her around, then picked her up and sat her on the countertop. Pushing her legs apart, I stood between them. "Or you gon' make me wanna violate you. I'm not trying to go there wit'chu, baby. Not yet anyway."

Her titties were right there, begging me to touch them. She saw me glance at them and I could feel her body shudder. Leaning my forehead against hers, I twirled her hair and held my other hand at her hip. Licking my lips, I finally backed away, then picked her up again. She wrapped her arms around my neck, as I allowed her body to slide down mine. Briefly closing my eyes, I grabbed her hand and led her to the bathroom. She'd never been past the kitchen.

I turned to go back to the front room, but she grabbed my shirt. Once that happened, I lost control for a minute. I pushed her against the wall and allowed my tongue to dive into her mouth. She looked a little caught off guard by my roughness, but quickly adjusted. She was playing with fire, and I knew for sure her ass wasn't ready for all this dick she was teasing. My hands roamed over her body again and squeezed her ass, when I got to it. She was so fucking sexy and she knew that shit.

I abruptly stopped groping her body and broke our kiss. Before she could stop me again, I took off for the front room, adjusting my dick as I walked. She wasn't little but I'd still break her ass in half. I could tell she wasn't as experienced as the ratchet ass females I used to deal with sometimes, and I was ready to take her places she'd only dreamed about during a wet dream.Wanting a woman this badly was new to me and trying to resist was unheard of.

I blew out an exasperated breath, as I sat on the couch. Kort-lynn went to her bag with a smirk on her lips. She knew she was getting me to the point of no return, but I didn't want her doing what she thought I wanted. Before heading back to the bathroom, she stood in front of me, then sat on my lap. I rubbed my hand down my face. Looking up at her, my hands began roaming again. Looking at her big ass titties in my face, I mumbled, "Why you torturing me?" Biting my bottom lip, I ran my fingertips over her cleavage.

"Zay, I'm tired of fighting how I feel. I told you that I was gonna do what I felt and whatever happened, happened."

"You sure about that? I don't want you to regret anything I do to this sexy ass body. Why don't you go take your shower, then we'll do whatever you want. That'll give you time to think about what you doing and make sure that's what you want. Deal?"

"Okay."

She stood from my lap, then went to the bathroom. I couldn't help but stroke my dick a couple of times. That nigga was out and ready to prowl. Once he came out of these shorts, there wouldn't be any stopping him. I hope she knew that. Trying to allow my body to relax, I started watching a rodeo on TV. Sometimes, I missed that shit and other times, not so much. Red had been trying to convince me to get into team roping with him. It was the event where two cowboys chased a steer and one roped the horns and the other roped the heels. Red could rope the horns with his eyes closed and I'd always been a decent heeler.

I'd practiced with him, a couple of times, when he was thinking about participating in the event. When he saw how good I was at it, with little practice, he said he wouldn't compete in that event without me. So, for the past two years, he'd been hounding me about it. He'd even offered to pay my entry fees, if that was what was holding me back. That shit was a gamble. Entry fees weren't cheap and if you didn't win, it was a loss. I wasn't broke, but I wasn't balling out of control, like Red and Legend either.

Not to mention, all the time I would have to put into practicing and actually going to the rodeos. It would take time away from me training and breaking horses, my only income. I made a comfortable living, and had a little money saved up. So, maybe I would take him up on that, one day, and see how it goes. If he was paying the entry fees, that would be a load off of me. Then, I would just have to concentrate on how to manage my time effectively. I wouldn't be able to do what I did today.

As I continued watching the rodeo, I heard the bathroom door open. She'd been in there over thirty minutes, but when she came within view, I couldn't help but bite my bottom lip. She wore some leggings and a t-shirt, nothing extravagant, but I could also see that she wasn't wearing a bra. Her nipples were hard as hell and I just wanted them in my mouth, like immediately. She walked over to the couch and just stood there, staring at me, as I licked my lips. My dick was hardening again and there wasn't a thing I could do to stop it.

Before I could say a word, she sat next to me. I knew she was contemplating what she would do but, chose the safer route. "So, what are you watching?"

"You," I said while sliding my fingertips from her shoulder to her hand.

I could feel the tremble that surged through her body, at my touch. She turned to me and the fire I saw in her beautiful eyes surprised me. I just knew she'd gotten cold feet. Throwing her leg across my body, she straddled me and kissed me deeply. *Hell fucking yeah.* My hands squeezed her ass. But before I got carried away, I needed to clear up some things. She kissed my lips and I almost lost focus, as her nails grazed the back of my head and my neck. "Listen. If we cross into this territory, ain't no going back. If my dick come out of these shorts, I ain't tryna hear you change your mind."

She stared at me, seriously, without saying a word, like she was going over my words in her head. "I want you bad, Kort. But I ain't a nigga for the back and forth. If I have you, I'm gon' keep having you. If there are problems, we gon' work shit out like adults. I don't care for unnecessary drama. You got me, baby?"

She nodded her head, then pulled her shirt over her head. I latched on to them nipples so damn fast, could've sworn I was a hungry newborn baby and she had milk. The moan that left those lips, set me ablaze. She was holding my head to her chest, like I was gonna get away. Shit, I wasn't going no damn where, now, and she was running out of time to change her mind. I slid my hands inside her tights, as she flinched. Pulling away from her, I had her stand to her feet, then stood and pulled her in my arms. I lifted her in my arms, and I could see the surprise in her eyes, every time I did.

I was six-five and two hundred sixty pounds. She had to know that I would have no issue picking her up. I walked to my bedroom and laid her in the bed and took off my shirt. Joining her, I continued kissing her wherever my lips landed. Kortlynn wrapped her legs around my waist and that shit was it. I stood and began pulling at her tights. Surprisingly, she didn't resist. As I stared at her, I could sense she was getting uncomfortable. "Damn, girl. You so beautiful."

I got on my knees and spread her legs. The juices present there were begging me to slurp that shit up and that's just what a nigga did. I made love to that fat pussy, with my tongue, making sure it touched every part of her before circling that juicy clit. As she panted, I stopped and laid in the bed. "Come sit on my face, Kort."

"What?"

Her eyes were wide. "What y'all say? If he dies, he dies? Bring yo' ass up here, girl. I'ma real man and can handle whatever you got to offer me. Bring that pussy here."

She hesitantly straddled my face like she was scared but, the minute I pulled her down, she moaned loudly. I hadn't eaten pussy in a long ass time but, when I tasted her, that shit came back to me quick, fast and in a hurry. She was so fucking hot and juicing so much that shit was rolling down my cheeks and had me sweating bullets. But, it tasted so damn good, I couldn't stop. "Ahh, Zay! I'm about to cum!"

Talk about her moans were sexy as hell. I sucked her clit even harder, begging for her sweet nectar to fill me up and drown my ass at the same time. I dove in deeper, literally not breathing, just to get her there, and she started grinding on my face then shot that shit everywhere. "Fuck!" she screamed as she tried to get away.

I took the opportunity to get a deep breath, then pulled her to me, still feasting on her shit. Once her body had relaxed more, I allowed her to fall on my bed. Shit, I was drenched in sweat, but I'd do that shit again, as soon as I could wipe my face. Going to my nightstand, I grabbed a condom, then went to the bathroom to clean my face. I'd test her level of freakiness another time. When I came back, she was in the same position, still panting. She looked over at me and, when she saw my dick, her eyes widened slightly.

I smiled at her, then tore open the condom. She sat up, leaning on her elbows to watch me. This shit wasn't the normal sized dick. I had some hang time, and before long, Kort was gon' be wondering whether it was me fucking her or one of them damn horses outside. She licked her lips as I made my way to her. I couldn't help but lick the residue from her pussy beforehand. Kissing, licking and sucking my way up her body, when I got to her face, I hesitated. I didn't know if she was cool with tasting herself, until she pulled my face to her and tongued the shit out of me.

I wanted to be gentle with her, since I knew it had been a while, but this beast she was pulling out of me wasn't having it. Lining up with her opening, I pushed inside of her. Not slowly but not quickly either. She yelled, "Oh, fuck!"

Sex had a way of bringing out her dutty mouth and I loved that shit. Biting her earlobe and kissing her neck, while my dick marinated inside that pussy, was so much torture. Her walls had me in a tight cocoon and I never wanted to become a butterfly. "You aight, baby?"

"Hell, yes. Damn, Zay. I had no idea. Shiiiit."

I smirked at her, then began stroking her. "Ahh, fuck, Kort. This is everything I thought it was gon' be," I said in her ear.

Going up on my knees, Kortlynn started screaming obscenities loudly. But when I felt her juices hitting my thighs, I knew why. She was squirting. *Oh, my God.* She was a fucking dream come true. "Fuck, girl."

When I realized she was cool, I began rough stroking her, giving her the shit I been wanting to give her. Grunting the entire time, I knew I was gonna cum quick as hell. It had been months since I'd dug in some pussy and even longer since I'd had some this good. "I'm cumming again, Zayson! Oh, my God!"

"I'm about to nut, too."

I dug in her shit until I couldn't go any deeper, then released the shit I'd been holding, in that latex. "Ahh, fuck!"

Yelling wasn't really my thing, but I couldn't help that shit. That Hoover had fucking sucked my shit dry. I was gon' need a minute to recuperate. When I slid out of her, the condom was full as hell, hanging off my dick. I pulled it off and showed it to her. "See what you did to me?"

She smiled lazily, then turned on her side. "That was amazing."

"Don't get proper, now. That shit was good as fuck."

She giggled. "Hell, yeah."

Chapter Eleven

K ortlynn

THIS COULDN'T BE A SIN, 'CAUSE, MY GOD! I FELT LIKE I WAS IN Heaven. Zay had pleased me beyond my wildest desires. He knew how to wait for me to adjust and, while he was fucking me, it felt like he was loving me at the same damn time. I'd came more times than I could count and for the first time ever, I squirted. After about a ten-minute break, we went at it again and I realized I was gon' have to start working out for sure, because I was tired as hell. When he noticed how tired I was, after round two, he laid me on my stomach and said, "I got'chu. Just toot it up for me."

And that I did, several times. It was like he couldn't get enough. I didn't want to stop but my body was telling me to cease and desist, immediately. We'd been laying in the bed for an hour, when I thought I'd gained enough strength to take another shower. It was only seven, but I knew if I laid here any longer, I was gonna be out.

Zayson was laying next to me, playing in my hair. "How long has it been since you had sex, baby?"

"Five years."

His eyes nearly popped out of their sockets. I giggled, as he sat up in bed. "Damn. For real?"

"Yeah. I decided to choose me. And if the men approaching me didn't think I was good enough to claim as theirs, then they weren't good enough to obtain my most prized possession. You are the first man that has wooed me until I couldn't really control my emotions. Something about you makes me wanna do all sorts of things."

"I can't believe I'm the first to acknowledge your worth. If I could give you the world, I'd give you that shit in a heartbeat. So, what sort of things you wanna do?"

"Don't take this the wrong way, but I definitely *want* to work out now. I need to be able to keep up with you. I was tired long before you were."

He ran his fingertips down my chest. "I'll help you, if you want. What you eat can play a factor in your energy level and stamina, too. So, make sure you drink plenty of water and get your vegetable intake up. Plus, the more we engage in these types of activities, your body will get used to it." He pulled me on top of him, and I immediately tensed up. "Relax, girl. Haven't I proven that your weight ain't shit to me?"

"Yeah. Sorry."

I relaxed and laid on his chest and it was the best feeling in the world. I'd never had a man to cherish me the way Zayson did. "So, when do you work out?"

"Usually in the evenings. I have a room, here, with weights, a treadmill and a bicycle. I hated going to the gym, so I made my own."

"Why did you hate going to the gym?"

"It was out of my way. If I don't wanna leave China, then I don't have to. You feel me?"

"Yep. I'm gonna need another shower."

"You sure you don't wanna wait until the morning? I might be tempted to eat that pussy again. It's on my mind, now, so if you come out the shower smelling all sweet again, I know I'm going down."

He slid his hands down my back and grabbed my ass. The fact that he couldn't seem to keep his hands off me made me giddy with excitement. Not only that, but he wanted to be with me in public, and it was genuine. Ain't shit feel better than being appreciated, valued and adored. As we had a quiet moment, I heard my phone vibrating. The only person that called me was my mother, and I wasn't trying to talk to her right now. All she would do is ruin my high. Every now and then, my dad and J'Neka called. Whomever it was, I'd call them back, because I just wanted to enjoy Zayson.

We continued to lay there, quietly, while he caressed my back. "So, if I take a shower in the morning, will I be safe?"

"Probably not."

He chuckled as I rolled off him. "Well, come on. You need a shower, too."

"Girl, don't threaten me with a good time."

My mind immediately said, *I'm too big to be trying to fuck in the shower.* I corralled my thoughts and stood to my feet. It felt like every muscle in my body was sore. I felt like an old woman. When we walked in the bathroom, Zayson went to the tub and started the water running and poured some lavender Epsom salt in there. I smiled at him. He was so thoughtful. Not having to ask showed that he paid attention to me. Hugging him from behind, he chuckled. "I'll put the desire to fuck you up in this shower on hold for another day. I'm still gon' eat that pussy when we get through, though. So, get yo' mind ready for that."

I smiled brightly, as I laid my head on his back. "Thank you, Zayson. You're so good to me."

He turned around and hugged me tightly, then kissed my head. When he released me, he went back to the room and came back with my phone. It was vibrating and the caller ID said Calvin. Zayson had a slight frown on his face and was staring at me. *Aww. He was already protective.* I answered on speaker, "Hey, Daddy."

"Hey, Kortlynn. How was your day?"

"It was good. What about yours?"

"Well, there's something I need to talk to you about. I actually need your help."

I frowned, slightly, as Zayson turned the water off in the tub and started it in his walk-in shower. "What's going on, Daddy?"

"I... uh... I have colon cancer. It's in stage three, so they wanna be aggressive with my treatment."

My heart sank. While I wasn't super close to him, I loved him, and I would do whatever I could to help him. Zayson was standing next to me, rubbing my back. "I'm so sorry. What do you need from me?"

"You're my only child, here in Beaumont, and the only person I feel like I can count on, besides my brother. I'll need someone to pick me up from chemo and radiation treatment and bring me home."

I had a brother that lived in California, that I knew about, but we'd never met. He and daddy weren't close at all and didn't have much of a relationship either. They only talked like once a month and that was because Daddy called him. He and I had only talked a few times, but we were aware of one another. He didn't give the vibe that he wanted a relationship with me either, so I let him be. "Of course. Will anyone be there with you?"

"No, baby. Everyone has to work. I understand that."

"What days will you have to go? I can always take one day a week to sit with you. What about Mom?"

"I called her, but she pretty much told me to go to hell."

"Ugh!"

How could she turn her back on him, at a time like this? Yes, they'd had a rough patch, but that was over twenty years ago. I was so disgusted with her. My daddy could die and that made me want to bond with him even more, before I no longer had him. "Don't worry, Kortlynn. Out of Monday and Thursday, what's your least busy day?"

"I have meetings on Thursdays, but they are usually over by ten. Mondays are the busiest."

"Okay. On Thursdays, I will be going at nine. You can just meet me there."

"I will change the meeting time to eight, that way I can be done by nine. I love you, Daddy, and whatever I can do to make this easier, I will."

"Thank you, baby. I love you, too. I'll call you Wednesday. Today was my first day, so my brother took off to be with me, but I knew I couldn't ask him to do that. Your job is a little more flexible than his."

"Daddy, I'll be checking on you more often, so you'll hear from me tomorrow. Okay?"

"Okay. Talk to you tomorrow."

I ended the call and just kind of stared off for a moment. Zayson pulled me to him. "You okay?"

"Umm... yeah."

I was trying to come to grips with what I just heard, but I couldn't seem to process it. Looking at my phone, I realized he'd been the one that had been trying to call me. Guilt flooded my being. From now on, I would at least look to see who was calling, no matter what. Slowly, I walked to the tub, and slid down in the hot water, as Zayson watched me closely. I suppose he was waiting for the tears to come, but they wouldn't. My whole life, I'd had to be strong, so I only had fleeting moments of weakness and that was usually when I was alone. And, even then, tears rarely came. It was the way my mom raised me. *As a fat girl, people are always going to have something negative to say. Develop tough skin and deal with it.* And that was what I did. I dealt with it the best way I knew how. It wasn't until I was a grown up that I actually started loving myself and said to hell with anyone who didn't like it.

Zay finally got in the shower and I closed my eyes. *My daddy has colon cancer.* I tried to put it out of my mind and just relax in the hot water. My body was tense, and I needed to relax before I gave myself a headache. Taking a few deep breaths, I opened my eyes and began washing myself, trying to avoid Zayson's sympathetic eyes. Hopefully, he didn't change his plans because of the news I'd gotten. I needed some time to get this off my mind, until I could clearly analyze the situation without the shock of it all.

⚜

"Why didn't you tell me my dad has cancer?"

"I figured he would call you. I was shocked he called me before talking to you, in the first place."

"You told him to go to hell, Mom?"

"I told him to find someone else to cater to his needs, because I wasn't the one for that job."

"Mom, he has cancer."

"And what does that have to do with me, Kortlynn? We haven't been on speaking terms since before you were born. We only spoke when you were ten, because I knew it would benefit you to have a connection with him. Now that you'll be taking care of him, you'll have so much to gain when he dies."

"Mary Hebert! Can you be any more insensitive?! I'm pretty much his only child and he isn't married. Not that any of that is important. I form relationships with people because I'm a genuinely loving person. What I can get out of them never comes to my mind, because I do a damn good job at providing for myself."

"Which means that this man you're messing around with is probably broke. And watch your tone with me, Kortlynn Denise. I don't like your father. That isn't a secret. It never has been. That hasn't changed because he has cancer. Now, are we done with this conversation?"

"Completely. Goodbye, Mom."

I ended the call, as I gritted my teeth. My good mood was long gone, and it seemed she could always take me there. Zayson had been great to me and for me. That night, after my bath, he'd given me a massage, then ate me out like I was his favorite dessert. But, the best part was him holding me in his arms the entire night. There wasn't a moment where he wasn't grasping for me to pull me back to him when I'd tossed and turned my way out of his embrace.

The next day, I didn't talk to my mother, at all, because I was too angry at what my dad had told me she said. I'd spoken to him, though, and he sounded happy that I'd called. I'd even gone to his house when I got off. I'd only gotten to see Zayson, briefly, when he brought me lunch and watered his crop. We'd also talked that night until I got sleepy. But, here it was Wednesday and I couldn't resist answering her phone call, although I knew that the conversation would go just the way it did; to hell in a handbasket.

I grabbed my purse to get ready to head out for lunch, just as a delivery guy approached my door. He was holding a beautiful bouquet of purple tulips with a huge purple bow. They literally took my breath away. After thanking the delivery guy, I called Zayson. "Baby, these flowers are beautiful!"

"Huh?"

"The flowers you sent me."

"I didn't send you any flowers, today, baby. You have some coming Friday, though."

Hmm. Who else could be sending me flowers? I never even thought to read the card, because Zayson was the only person I expected to receive flowers from. I opened the card to read, *I hope you're having a great day. Love, your dad.* I could feel the tears forming, but I swallowed them back and cleared my throat. He remembered I liked tulips. "They were from my daddy. I didn't read the card, I just assumed they were from you."

"Oh, okay. I thought I was gonna have to whoop somebody's ass. Kortlynn Denise Hebert is all mine, now. Everybody else had all the time in the world to make a move. Time's up."

I giggled, then admired the flowers once more. Leaving them on my desk, I walked out of my office to go home and eat. Zayson and I had come up with a healthier menu for me and I'd gone to the store, when I left my dad yesterday. I'd grilled chicken breast, steamed vegetables and boiled potatoes. Today would be my first day, and I would also be working out with him, when I got off from work. "I'm all yours and you're all mine. You're everything I want in a man. Thank God Legend gave you my number."

"I know. Speaking of Legend, he and Red have been trying to get me back into rodeoing, team roping with Red. What'chu think about that?"

"I think I'll support you in whatever you want to do. I don't have a clue about rodeoing, so I just know that if you're doing it, I'll be there."

"Damn. You gon' ride for me like that?"

"Yeah. You'd do the same for me, right?"

"Hell yeah. Without question."

"Okay, then. If you think it's something you wanna try again, I'm here for it. Even if that means I gotta see my big head cousin more often."

He chuckled. "Yeah, 'cause we'd have to practice. What'chu doing?"

"I'm on my way home, to eat lunch. I didn't want to bring it with me. Getting used to Serita being back has been a little harder than what I thought it would be, so I figured I needed to just get away for lunch."

We continued to talk a little while longer, until I'd walked inside my place, then I promised to see him later, to workout. I was so used to doing what I wanted to do, coming and going as I pleased, it was hard to work for someone again, within the same environment. Her sister, Sidney had been back, as well as her other sister, Shannon, and they'd pretty much stayed cooped up in her office. I didn't feel included and I just hoped I wouldn't be left out. She'd said I would be the assistant director, so hopefully she didn't change her mind on that.

Sidney had her own practice and Shannon had an interior design business she was running. So, I knew she wouldn't be giving them my position. Working with the girls was something I loved. Regardless of pay, if she left me out, I wouldn't be happy. I'd been strictly doing paperwork all day. I could push a pen anywhere. Taking a deep breath, I took out my lunch and put it in the microwave. As I waited, I decided to text my dad. *Thank you so much for the flowers. They're beautiful.*

Just like you. You're welcome.

I smiled at his message, then ate lunch. Trying to focus my mind on Zayson and his possible venture into rodeoing again, I looked up team roping on my phone. He was gonna make me a country girl before it was all over.

Chapter Twelve

Z ayson

"COME ON, BABY GIRL. TWO MORE. YOU'RE DOING SO GOOD."

We were in my workout room, at my house, and Kortlynn was working her legs out on one of the machines. She only had two more reps to do. Baby girl was tired, and she was sweating profusely. After walking for thirty minutes, she'd been trying out the different weight machines. Once she did these last two reps, she'd be done. "Zay, I'm tapped out."

"This is all you have left, baby. Don't quit when you're so close to finishing. You can do it."

I stood in front of her, for a moment, letting her see my eyes. Kissing her lips, I used the towel on my shoulder to wipe her face, then stepped aside again. She dug in and did one, then growled her way through the last one. When she did, I lifted her from the machine and hugged her tightly. "You did so good, baby. I'm proud of you."

"Zayson. This was hard."

"I know, baby. It'll get easier, though."

I let her go, so she could sit on the bench while I went to run her bath water. She'd put some serious work in. I just truly hoped she was doing this for herself and no one else. After sprinkling her Epsom salt in the tub, I went back to get her. When I walked in, I couldn't help but smile. She was laying on the workout bench, with her arms stretched up over her head. "Come on, baby, so I can bathe you."

I grabbed her hand and helped her up. "I can clean myself, Zay. But if you don't mind, I could really use a massage afterwards."

"Don't worry, I got'chu."

After she slid down in the hot water, I went to the front and called my mama. She'd called while we were working out, so I didn't want to stop to answer. The minute she answered the phone, she went in. "Yo' raggedy ass brother came here, and I almost stabbed him in his lying ass thoat."

I dropped my head. It was always some fucking drama with Kerry. I didn't understand why he couldn't get his shit together. "What did he say, Ma?"

"In so many words, to mind our damn business and that when that horse won, he would pay us our money. But I know I can kiss that money goodbye. We ain't gon' ever get it. It's gon' be a blizzard in hell before he get anything else from us. I swear, I don't know where we went wrong with Kerry. Usually, it's the youngest that's spoiled rotten and won't do right. But this nigga proves that theory wrong every time he opens his mouth."

"Well, Ma, at this point, all you can do is move on. If he comes around, after this, then, cool. If he doesn't, that's cool, too."

"It will never be cool to not see my son, Zay. I'm angry and I want to beat his ass, but that's still my son. He's always welcome at my house. He would have to do something a lot worse than this for him not to be welcomed. It just hurts that he treats us the way he does. It hurts your daddy, too."

I could hear her voice quiver. "Don't cry, Ma. Just pray for him. That's all you can do."

"You right, baby. Well, I'll let you go. Tell my girl I said hello."

"I will, as soon as she's done with her bath."

"Bath? Oh, shit. Y'all done went to a new level and you just now spilling the beans?"

"Aww, hell. There you go."

"I see y'all. That's gon' be my daughter-in-law. Tell her to call me."

"I will do no such thing. Good night, Barbara."

"Bye, boy."

Kerry was really fucking up. I didn't see how he could disrespect them the way he did. Our parents had been good to us and they didn't deserve the cold shoulder from him or his hateful words. Once Kortlynn left, tomorrow, I would call him and tell him about himself. Before I could go to the bathroom, to check on my baby and to take a shower, a car pulled in my driveway. Looking out the window, I saw it was Kerry's bitch ass. *Shit!* I didn't feel like talking to his ass right now.

I went outside and sat in the rocking chair. He didn't need to be in the house, just in case baby girl came out of that bathroom in something just for me. I watched him slam his car door and walk to my porch. "I guess yo' mama called you," he said from afar.

"Yep."

I shook his hand when he got close, then he sat in the chair next to me. "Who's here?" he asked, just as Kortlynn opened the door.

She had her keys in her hand, so I assumed she needed something from her car. She unlocked it with her key fob, then smiled at my brother. "I'll be right back," she said.

When she came back, I'd make the introductions, although I really didn't want to. Kerry was so damn shallow. He didn't have a woman, nor could he keep one, but he always had the nerve to tell me the shit I was doing wrong regarding women. Like he was the damn relationship expert. "Damn, she a big bitch."

Before he could count to three, I was on his ass. I'd yanked his ass out of that chair and held him by his shirt, against the house. "You gon' watch yo' fucking mouth."

"Nigga, you better let my shirt go. Sensitive ass. That's why you ain't got a girl yet. So, you had to settle for the bottom of the barrel."

That was it. I knocked his ass out, then turned to see Kortlynn standing there, eyes wide. Kerry dropped to the ground like a sack of potatoes. I walked to Kortlynn. "I'm sorry you had to witness that. He's my brother. While I love him, I can't stand his ass sometimes. Today is one of those times."

"I heard what he said. I'm used to the insults. That doesn't crush my spirit anymore. So, you didn't have to do that, on account of me."

"I need him to know that he will not disrespect you. Regardless of what you can handle, emotionally, he needs to respect you for the beautiful, intelligent woman that you are. If he can't, he gon' catch these hands every time."

She rubbed my cheek, then grabbed my hand. It was red, but that wasn't something I wasn't used to dealing with. Shit, I lived in the country and had a miniature-sized farm I was running. So, that shit was minute. She smiled softly at me, then lifted my hand to her lips and kissed it softly. I couldn't help but reciprocate, as I heard that nigga coming to on the porch. Kortlynn wrapped her arms around my one arm. Either she was trying to restrain me or protect herself. Kerry stood and stumbled a bit, then looked at me. Slowly, I walked to the porch, not taking my eyes off him.

He sat in the rocking chair, I assume to get his bearings, as I opened the door for Kortlynn to go inside. Once she did, I looked at him and said, "Get the fuck off my porch."

He stood and looked me in my eyes, like he wanted to do something. I was ready for whatever, because I'd lay him on his fucking back again. I'd forgotten all about getting on his ass about how he talked to and treated our parents. He slowly began walking away, then said, "She won't be any different. You ain't shit and soon she gon' realize that. Big or small, you can't keep them."

I wanted to run off this porch and just beat the shit out of his ass but, when I felt her touch, I knew it was best that I just let his ass leave. He was miserable and misery could go keep company with somebody else. Following her inside, I closed the door behind me, then pulled her in my arms. "I'm sorry for his ignorant ass. It wasn't that I couldn't keep a woman. I just hadn't met you yet."

"Oh, yeah? Well, I feel better after my bath. I could use another workout."

"You think you can handle it?" I asked, roughly pulling her closer.

My dick was hard, that fast, and was ready to tear some shit up. "I can handle whatever. You just gotta dish it out."

"We gon' see."

I picked her up and kissed her passionately, thankful for everything about her beautiful ass, and carried her to the room. "I'm 'bout to get real nasty with you. You gon' have to take another bath and soak in Epsom salt again. Now, be a good girl and spread them legs for daddy."

❧

"NAW, HE BROUGHT HIS ASS HERE TO PROBABLY TELL ME ABOUT what happened between y'all, but insulted Kortlynn, the minute he saw her. I wanted to really fuck him up. He better be glad he my brother or he woulda got more."

I was on the phone with my daddy, explaining what had happened with Kerry, yesterday. Small town gossip had gotten to him. "You did the right thing by standing up for your woman, son. Don't ever let anybody disrespect her."

"You don't have to worry about that. I'll go to jail before I let that happen."

"You love her, don't you?"

"I wouldn't say love, but I really care for her a lot."

"I can tell. Where are you?"

"I'm on my way to bring her lunch. She's with her dad, for his chemo and radiation treatment."

"Oh. I didn't know her dad had cancer."

"She just found out Monday, I think."

"Oh. Well, tell her that we wishing for the best."

"I'll tell her. Talk to you later, old man."

"Okay. Bye."

I was halfway expecting for my mama to call me, about what happened between me and Kerry, not my daddy. She was crying about that shit he did to them yesterday and that hurt my heart. When I got back from Beaumont, I'd go check on her. It had been a full fucking day already. I'd taken care of Kortlynn proper-like last night. Had her sucking her juices from my fingers and all kinds of nasty shit she was down for. She sucked my dick like she was trying to get that throat real lubricated. I didn't let her finish, though, because I couldn't take the way she was teasing me.

We'd fucked her soreness right back in them muscles. She had to get up early just to soak again. Kortlynn was all hunched over and shit. I couldn't help but laugh. So, while she was soaking, I went and got some work in on that colt. By the time she left, at seven-thirty, I was already a sweaty mess, getting bucked and worked hard as hell. Kortlynn got to see a little bit of it and she looked amazed that I could stay on a bucking horse. I'd gotten off and kissed her bye, then went back to work.

When I got to the treatment center, with Kortlynn's lunch, it was almost noon. I knew baby girl was hungry, but I'd gotten behind on training the colt. I'd lost track of time. I texted her and let her know I was outside, so she came and met me. "I'm sorry I'm late, baby."

"It's okay. I had some crackers to snack on. Zay, do you have plans tomorrow evening?"

"Not unless you do," I said, then smirked as she laughed.

That was the same thing she'd told me, a while back. "I want you to meet my mom. Well, not really, but she wants to meet you."

"Why you don't want me to meet your mom," I asked while pulling her in my arms.

"Because she can be so bougie and judgmental at times. There are times that I don't want to be around her. But the good thing is that Legend's mom will be there. She knows you already, right?"

"Yeah. I've met Mrs. Semien a few times. Now, you might get a little jealous, 'cause she always flirts with me. I told her she had better quit before Legend be calling me daddy. That just made it worse."

Kortlynn laughed loudly. "That sounds like my Aunt Rose. Well, I better get back inside. Talk to you later."

"Aight, baby."

I kissed her lips, then went by the center to water the bell peppers. I didn't want to just go back there without anyone knowing I was here, so I went inside to where I knew Serita's office was. Before I could knock, I could hear a conversation going on and Serita had gotten a little loud. She said, "If I didn't think I could handle it, I wouldn't be here."

Someone else said, "The stress of running this place, plus losing Shawn is what got you hooked."

"Sidney, you're forgetting one important piece. Reginald's trifling ass. Had it not been for him, I would have never thought about snorting cocaine. Using had never crossed my mind, not even smoking a damn cigarette."

I stepped away from the door, some, until I heard Kortlynn's name. "I told her I would keep her on, with the same pay."

"How will you do that, Serita? The center lost some of its funding when you left. Kortlynn is a great person, but either you're gonna have to cut her pay significantly or you won't be coming back as the director. And, technically, you need an income. So, you're going to have to decide, soon, what you're gonna do. Shawn's generosity is going to run out and I believe Sonya will make sure it does. He's your ex-husband and your three kids with him are practically grown. Kyla is almost done with her junior year. After her, what allegiance do any of them owe you?"

"Shit! I can't do that to Kortlynn. I gave her my word."

"Then go find another job, Serita."

Fuck! She was gonna let my baby go. I knocked on the door, and everything got quiet. After a moment, Serita opened the door and her face got red as hell. "Hello, Serita. I just wanted to let you know I would be in back, watering the crop. I didn't wanna just go back there without anyone knowing I was here."

"Oh... Oh, okay. Thanks."

I smiled a little, then walked away. Warning Kortlynn was the first thing on my mind, but I got a flashback of last time. I didn't want to upset her, but at the same time, I didn't want her to get blindsided. Taking a deep breath, I decided to give it time. I was almost sure Serita wouldn't do this right away. She seemed to be genuinely looking out for Kortlynn. After watering the crop and fertilizing it, I headed home to go talk to Queen Ardoin.

Chapter Thirteen

K ortlynn

WATCHING DADDY IN SO MUCH PAIN HAD HURT ME BEYOND belief. I didn't think it was this bad. He'd done well, hiding his pain from me the day I just visited, but I was with him so long yesterday during his treatment, he couldn't hide it. After assuring him that I could handle it, he relaxed some and became something I'd never seen him be.

Weak.

Dependent.

Vulnerable.

It was hard, but I didn't want him trying to play tough, in front of me, making himself feel worse. Serita had let me leave early. I needed to get a massage to relax my nerves before dinner tonight. I had a feeling that Mary was gon' show her ass. I just had that feeling. What she had no clue about, was that I would defend Zayson with everything in me and would leave that dinner with the quickness. Just like he stood up for me, with his brother, I would do the same with my mother. I wouldn't physically touch my mother, but she wouldn't dare get away with disrespecting him.

As I headed home to take a bath, my cell phone started to ring. Looking at the caller ID, I saw it was my cousin J'Neka. "Hello?"

"Hey! Guess who just graced Beaumont with her presence."

I giggled. She was something else. "I'm gonna take a wild guess and say... I don't know... you?"

Neka laughed loudly. "So, what's the deal? I'm ready to turn the hell up! I was so stressed for finals."

"Well, your Aunt Mary is cooking dinner because she wants to meet Zay."

"Aww, shit. I will definitely be there for that. What time?"

"At six. Aunt Rose will be there, too. Hopefully, she brings rein-forcement, too."

"Shit, I hope so. I always thought that the reason guys didn't hang around long was because of Aunt Mary. She's so protective of you, sometimes. At least that's what I originally thought. Then, I realized that she has a problem with your weight and thinks everyone else does, too."

Well, damn. She just analyzed the hell out of Mary. Playing the fool, I asked, "You think so?"

"I don't think so, I know so. I can't wait to meet Zayson. He got your nose wide open. You can park a damn bus in there."

"Shut the hell up, Neka." I blew out a hard breath. "I think I've fallen for him."

"Shut the hell up! For real?"

"Yeah. I refuse to say anything to him about it, though. I don't want him to feel pressured into saying it back. I love his country ass."

She laughed. "Country?"

"Yes. Country. He trains horses for a living and watches the rodeo on TV, not to mention Tombstone. He watches it over and over. The intriguing part, though, is that he got just the right amount of hood in him. If you saw him around Beaumont, you wouldn't know just how country he was."

"So, he ain't wearing no cowboy boots, Wranglers and a cowboy hat?"

"Most times, he has on a baseball hat and tennis shoes. And he sure in the hell ain't wearing Wranglers. He so sexy, Neka. My body responds to his voice like you wouldn't believe."

"He just have the kitty purring. I'm excited for you. Well, let me get cleaned up and dressed so I won't miss this. Legend gon' be there?"

"Probably not. His wife might be, since her and Aunt Rose are close."

"Oh, okay. Well, see you later, girl. Hopefully, Aunt Mary behaves herself."

"Yeah. Hopefully."

I ended the call and went inside my apartment. Thinking about what J'Neka said was gonna put me in a foul mood and on guard, but here I was thinking about the shit. I'd only brought three guys home to meet my mama. She didn't like any of them. Not long after, we'd break up. They were different time ranges, but none of them were over three months. Then, she would say, *I told you they weren't worth your time.*

I'd agree with her and sulk about not being able to keep a boyfriend, no matter how great my personality was. None of them had ever complained about my mother, so I never pinpointed what she was doing. With the last breakup, I'd cried and stayed cooped in my apartment the whole weekend, eating ice cream. It seemed that I gained a good five pounds after each breakup. When I broke up with Marcus, the last boyfriend, I went through counseling and vowed to love myself before getting involved with anyone else.

I'd slipped up with Marcus about a year after that, and again five years ago, but that was it, until I'd met Zayson. And now I was in love with him. *Damn, Kort.* Here I was, the one trying to move slow, but I was the first one to fall in love. He was irresistible. There was nothing

I could have done to avoid the feelings I had for him. And, at this point, I was glad that I had the sense to run back to him before it was too late. The way I felt for Zayson, in just a short time, was crazy as hell to me. I'd never fallen so fast.

I just hoped my mother didn't threaten to ruin something so perfect. Zayson wanted me and I didn't think he was the type of man to let anybody keep him from what he wanted. Now that I had met him, I'd definitely become that woman. My mama had controlled my life long enough. Zayson had fixed my lonely, and it seemed like Mary needed somebody to fix hers. That was probably why she was so miserable. I slid down in the hot water and exhaled, trying to let Calgon take me away. Zayson would be meeting me here and I didn't want him to have to wait on me, so I didn't soak long.

Once I'd shaved my underarms and moisturized my skin with some skin care products made by a colleague of mine, the doorbell was ringing. It was only four. I frowned slightly, then put my robe on and slid into my house shoes. I hated walking bare footed, even in my own house. Zayson had found that to be funny. I told him everybody couldn't be country like his ass, walking bare footed on rocks and shit. He always got a kick out of my hood voice. I was always so proper, so when it came out, it usually caught him by surprise.

Trekking to the door, I checked the peephole to see Zayson standing there, looking fine as ever, in some white pants and a light pink shirt. He licked his lips, as he looked around, then looked back at the peephole. He smiled. "Come on, girl before I start sweating. I can see your eye through the peephole."

I smiled, then hurriedly opened the door. He walked in and closed it behind him, then pulled me to him, by the belt of my robe. "Come here, girl. I missed you."

He kissed me deeply before I could utter a response and tangled his fingers in my natural curls. The softness of his lips made parting from them that much harder, but somehow, I managed. "Hey, baby. I missed you, too."

"How much?" he asked, then bit his bottom lip.

"Zayson," I giggled, then continued. "It's already four. We can't be late."

"I'll be quick, for now, and take my time with you later. You gon' let this hard dick go to waste? He missed you, too."

I rolled my eyes, but I couldn't stop my hand from caressing it through his pants. He dropped his head back and groaned. I untied the belt of my robe, then allowed it to drop to the floor in a puddle and knelt on it. When I looked up at Zay, he was staring at me. I quickly undid his pants and pulled out the lady killer... the shit that had me walking with a slight limp when we were done... my guide for the scenic but informative tour it took me on.

It was like I didn't know my own body until his dick spoke to it and told it how to react to his greatness. The things it did in response to his slow, deep strokes were unspeakable, but the things my body did in response to his quick, but deadly strokes, was something to write about. Whenever he fucked me hard, I would squirt every-where. That only turned him on even more so. I slowly pulled the tip of his dick in my mouth and teased it with my tongue, then tried to swallow it whole. I knew that was impossible, but nothing could stop me from trying. "Oh, shit!"

Zayson slid his fingers through my hair and started a slow rhythm, in my mouth, that had me perfecting those suction skills. I would have dimples when I was done with him. Before long, he got impatient and started fucking my mouth, staring at me like I was engaging in an Oscar-worthy performance. Looking up at him, I could see him biting his lip with a deep frown on his face. He tried to slide out of my mouth, but I wasn't having it today. I needed to know how sweet his milk and honey was. "Kortlynn, fuck, girl. I'm about to cum. You sure you want this shit?"

I moaned on his shaft and kept my rhythm going, until he spewed in the back of my throat. Pulling away from it, a little, I savored his flavor before he yanked me from the floor and duck walked to my couch. Zay took off his white pants, carefully laying them across the chair. "Fuck!"

"What's wrong?"

"I didn't bring any condoms."

He began pulling up his drawers. "I'm on the pill. If you got a disease, I already swallowed the shit. Now cum pump me with that grade A shit."

Zayson didn't waste any time getting to me. I laid on my stomach and arched my back, just how he liked it. Lowering his head, he ate me out from the back and gave my ass some attention, too. "Zay, please, give it to me."

"You begging now?"

"Yes... that dick is worth every whine that falls from my lips. Put me out of my misery, baby. Pleeeaase..."

"Damn, girl. I'm glad you recognize this shit for what it is but, let me tell you about this fat ass pussy."

He slid inside of me and his body shuddered. "You felt that? Yo' shit wrap me up so damn tight, she almost cut off my circulation."

He pulled out and it made a pop noise. "You heard that shit? She suck a nigga in every time."

He reentered me and started stroking me. "Now, you hear that? She serenading a nigga. But, now, I'm 'bout to make her so fucking mad, she gon' spit at me."

With that statement, all talking ceased and he began destroying my insides, taking me to new places with every stroke. He pulled out of me, then made me stand up. He put my robe on the couch, then pushed me down and knelt between my legs. He pulled my hips to him. "You know I ain't ever wearing a fucking condom again. The way this shit feel, without that latex barrier, is something I can't let go of."

Zay shoved his shit inside of me, making me scream. Plummeting what had to be ten inches inside of me, he grabbed my breasts while I lifted my legs. He rested his hands on my inner thigh, then fucked me into paralysis. My mouth was formed into an O and I couldn't move. "Zay! You want it? I'm about to cum!"

Right after, I squirted on him, as he slowly shook his head. He fucked me harder, as he panted. The power he was giving me was gon' have me needing to soak again. "You muthafucka! Zayson James Ardoin!"

"Uh huh! Give me that hood shit."

He frowned so deeply, it looked like he was in pain, then he dropped his head to my chest. "Fuuuuck!"

He growled deeply and he scared the fuck out of me. Looking over his red skin, I knew this had been the ultimate shit for him. When he finally picked his head up, he kissed my lips, then slid out of me. "I'm gon' take a damn nap while you get ready. Yo' pussy done sucked the fucking life out a nigga. If I don't sleep this shit off, I won't be good for nothing else."

I giggled, then got up to get him a towel. That was amazing, but I had better make sure I took that pill faithfully. I couldn't be bringing no babies into the world just yet. I wanted to enjoy having him all to myself.

Chapter Fourteen

Z ayson

"It's nice to meet you, Jason."

I could see now, Kortlynn's mama was gon' make the nigga come out of me. "His name is Zayson, Mom," Kortlynn corrected.

"Oh. I'm so sorry. I thought she'd said Jason. Excuse me, Zayson. Have a seat."

"Did you say Zayson?"

I already knew that was Mrs. Semien. She'd yelled from the kitchen, as Ms. Hebert rolled her eyes. Before long, Kortlynn's Aunt Rose came running from the kitchen. "Hey, baby daddy!"

I picked her up as I hugged her, and she giggled like a little girl. "Kortlynn, I can't believe you tryna take my man."

"Don't make me call Legend," she said to her as they hugged.

"Leave his ass where he at." She paused, then yelled, "Harper?"

Harper was Legend's wife. I'd met her a couple of times. She walked out of the kitchen and smiled brightly. She hugged Kortlynn, then me. "I had to come make the dessert for one of my favorite women."

"What did you make?"

"My famous banana pudding cupcakes."

"Oh, my Lord. I'm cutting back and that's gon' kill it."

"He's already put you on a diet?" Mrs. Hebert said nastily.

I frowned, but before I could respond, Kortlynn said, "Come on, Mom, don't start. I'm doing this because I want to. Unlike most people, he appreciates me just the way I am."

I scanned her body, in that light pink wrap dress and just wanted to take her again, right here in her mother's house. I grabbed her hand and kissed her forehead, while her mother scrunched her nose. I saw what Kortlynn meant. She was as bougie as they came. The doorbell rang, so Mrs. Hebert went to answer it. A young woman walked in the room, so I stood to my feet. She screamed and she and Kortlynn embraced tightly. When they separated, Kort looked at me. "This is my cousin, J'Neka."

She extended her hand, so I shook it. I wasn't feeling her vibe. "Nice to meet you."

She smiled brightly and said, "Likewise."

Her eyes widened when she looked at Kortlynn and they laughed. It was going to be a long evening. I could see that shit already. I sat back in my seat, as Kortlynn and her cousin chattered away. Ms. Hebert was staring at me, though. I could see her from my peripheral. Grabbing Kortlynn's hand, I held it between mine, while she talked. When they'd gotten a break in conversation, Ms. Hebert asked, "So what do you do for a living, Jason?"

I refused to answer, but Kortlynn didn't have a problem addressing her. "Can I talk to you privately?"

"What for? We have guests."

"If you don't want to talk privately, I will say whatever I have to say in front of our guests."

Kortlynn's nostrils had flared. Her anger was about to overtake her, so I gently rubbed her hand. This situation wasn't going to get to me. I knew her mother was only doing that shit to get a rise out of me. But she wouldn't get it. However, I knew I wouldn't be coming back here no time soon. Her mother crossed her legs and stared at her, as if daring her to check her. Kortlynn didn't back down. "His name is Zayson. If you can't remember that, call him Mr. Ardoin."

Her mother frowned and, just as she was about to spew what I thought would be venom, Kortlynn continued. "Call him anything other than those two names again, and we will be out of here. You will respect him, and I won't tolerate you trying to belittle him. Period."

Mrs. Semien peeked her head out the kitchen. Her eyebrows were raised, and she had a slight smile on her lips. That almost made me laugh, so I turned my attention back to Kortlynn. I pulled her close to me. "It's okay, baby. I'm good. Don't get worked up, okay?"

"Did that advice work for you, the other day, with your brother?"

She was flaming hot. I nodded my head. "Aight. You got me."

"Kortlynn, come to the kitchen, please," her mother said.

"Why? I asked to talk to you privately, a minute ago, but you didn't want that. Come on, Zay. We can go to dinner somewhere else."

"Young lady! You will not disrespect me in my house! I didn't raise you that way."

"That's why we're leaving."

"Mary, if you don't sit'cho ass down. Kortlynn is a whole ass woman that you disrespect all the time but expect her to bow down to your ass. Shut the fuck up and let her live. And you gon' respect Zayson. He's a good man and the two of them are blessed to have each other. I'm in yo' house, so what'chu gotta say to me? I dare you."

Maaaaaan, everybody was quiet as hell. Mrs. Semien didn't play. Most times I was around her, she was always clowning, but there were those rare occasions, like now, that she had to shut shit down. "Kortlynn, please stay. Harper and I cooked for everybody to enjoy. Please?"

Kortlynn glanced at her mother, then back at Mrs. Semien and slowly sat. I put my arm around her, trying to ease her tension. Although, that split in that wrap dress was about to make me rough her ass up. It was already split to her knee, when she was standing, but when she sat, it revealed almost her entire thigh. Even though I'd gotten a taste before we got here, that wasn't nearly enough. Quickies with her only tortured me, making me want more. A nigga needed at least three nuts. I leaned in close to her and whispered in her ear. "Just relax, baby, and imagine all the things I'm gon' do to this sexy ass body tonight."

Instantly, I could feel a shift in her. She stared at me, then a smile made its way to her lips. "Thank you, baby."

"Zayson, tell me, do you have any fine brothers, cousins or friends I can hook up with?"

I looked over at Neka and I still didn't feel like she was being genuine. She wanted me. I frowned at her. "I don't know about fine, 'cause I don't look at dudes. I have a brother, though."

Yeah, I said that shit. Although Kerry got on my nerves, she deserved him. I could see, in her eyes, that she was on some fuck shit. "How old is he?"

"Thirty-seven."

Ms. Hebert stood from her seat, like she had been in a trance all that time and went to the kitchen. We all watched her and, the minute she went in there, J'Neka said, "I don't want no weak nigga, na."

"Well, you will have to be the judge of that."

Pulling Kortlynn closer, I nibbled on her ear while secretly watching Neka. The smile had faded from her face, as Kortlynn closed her eyes and enjoyed how I was making her feel. J'Neka turned her head the other way, then eventually went to the kitchen. "Baby, this dress is making me horny as fuck. All this cleavage and exposed thigh is making me wanna take you in a bathroom."

"Well, had Aunt Rose not stepped in, we could've gone to my place and worked our appetites up real good."

"You damn right. Let me kiss them pretty ass lips at least."

She lifted her head and I gave her a soft kiss and gently sucked her bottom lip. When I let it go, she rubbed her lips together, I assume trying to even out the lipstick I had sucked off. Before I could kiss her again, her mother stepped back in the room. She looked at Kortlynn. "I just want what's best for you. I'm going to be hard on your choices for a partner because I wanna see their true character and not the one they brought in here to try to impress me. So, excuse me for giving a damn about you."

"Mom, this has nothing to do with showing respect. You don't do disrespectful things to people and expect them to respect you in return. Zayson has not disrespected you and neither has anyone I've ever dated. The difference now is that we're both thirty plus. We are both tired of the games and just want to be with someone who wants the things we want. I found that in him. So, no matter how you act, he's gonna be here."

I continued to love on Kortlynn, my way, trying to keep her calm. My main way couldn't happen right now, so I just continued to gently caress her, kiss her cheek and hold her hand. She was my baby and I hated to see her upset or angry. Which was the reason why I wasn't gon' tell her that her no good cousin was staring at me, from the kitchen, with that "come fuck me" look on her face.

Chapter Fifteen

K ortlynn

IF MARY HEBERT WASN'T MY MOTHER, I WOULD'VE CURSED HER ass out. After our last exchange about Zayson, we didn't say another word to each other, until we were leaving. However, Aunt Rose said everything I wanted to say to her. *Just shut the fuck up sometimes.* It did make our love session that much more intense. Zay loved on me so good, I almost told him I loved him. The heat of passion was no joke. It had you admitting all kinds of shit.

It was good to see J'Neka. She was my ace, but I could tell she wanted Zay. Nothing about me was naïve, and I could see how she was looking at him when she thought I wasn't paying attention. I knew she was a sexual being, but I thought we had an understanding and a love for each other that went beyond shit like this. Peeping game was my forte. Shallow women somehow thought that if a fine ass nigga was with a big girl, he was settling. But I could show her ass better than I could tell her.

I knew that Zayson had seen it, too, especially when he said he would hook her up with his brother. His brother got on his damn nerves and he'd told me how childish and irresponsible he was. I gathered that much when he'd called me a big bitch. It was a shame how insensitive people could be toward one another. I would have had no problem speaking up for myself, had Zayson not done so. His brother looked more like their dad but had a big ass water head. His teeth were jacked up, too. So, Zay was exacting payback on both of them by hooking them up with each other. When he gave her Kerry's number, before we left, I could see the smirk on his lips.

Sitting at my desk, with the door open, I could hear Serita and her sister, Sidney, arguing. They'd been doing that a lot lately. For the past week, I'd been hearing them occasionally get loud with each other. I'd been sure to keep my distance, so I didn't get caught up in the crossfire. As I finished up the last of my paperwork, I decided to go look outside at my baby's crop. When I opened the door and walked around the building, I saw a green stem with two green bulbs on it. So, his test was a success and I couldn't be happier. Just as I was heading back inside, Zay sent a text. *I need to talk to you, baby.*

It felt like all the breath left my body. Usually, when someone said that, bad news followed. I responded with a simple, *Okay,* then headed back to my office. Before I could get there, Sidney walked out of Serita's office and slammed the door. She didn't acknowledge me at all. I didn't take it personally, though, because I knew some people were that way when they were angry. Going in my office, I closed the door, then proceeded to call my baby. "Hey, baby girl."

"Hey, baby. How's your day going?"

"Good. I just about have this colt completely broken."

"That's great, baby. So, what's going on?"

"Are you almost done at work?"

"Yeah. I'm about to leave. Are you gonna meet me at home?"

"I'm gonna meet you when you walk outside."

"Yay! You're here! I'm coming out now."

"Aight."

I grabbed my things and hurriedly left my office. Today had been extra slow and I was ready to get the weekend started. Last weekend, at my mother's house, hadn't been so great. So, this weekend, I planned to spend in China with my baby. We had Sunday dinner planned at his parents' house, again, and we were also supposed to be going to Red's house tomorrow. Today, we had plans to work out and cook at his house. It would be my first time eating his barbeque and I couldn't wait.

When I walked outside, Zay was sitting in his truck, waiting for me. Smiling big, I walked over to his window and kissed his lips. "You couldn't wait for me to get out there?"

"Hell naw. You know I wish I could spend all my time with you. So, the minute I'm free, I wanna be up under you... behind you... on top of you..."

"Zay, don't get me all worked up. Then, I won't want to work out."

He smiled brightly. "I'll follow you, baby."

"Okay."

When we got to my place, I was nervous. I knew whatever was on his mind is what had him drive out here to talk to me. He didn't seem nervous about anything, so hopefully this had nothing to do with our relationship. While I was a strong and independent woman, I was quickly realizing that I was getting more and more attached to Zayson. Just like he wanted to be with me, every waking moment, I wanted the same.

I got out of my car and headed to my apartment. By the time I got to the door and unlocked it, Zayson was standing close to me, causing all the hairs on my neck to stand. We walked inside and before I could put my purse down, he'd pulled me in his arms and kissed me passionately. Because I went with my dad, on Thursdays now, we didn't get to see one another. We could probably make time, but Zayson had said that he would give up his time to my dad for the whole day. As I began to pull on his shirt, he pulled away from me and led me to the couch.

This had to be serious, because Zayson never stopped me when I wanted to get at him. I kept glancing at his hard dick, and he laughed, then held my head up. "If I didn't know any better, I'd think you wanted to attack me, right now, girl."

"I do. Shit."

Pulling his face to mine again, I kissed him hungrily, as he pulled me astride his lap. *Hell yeah.* I pulled my Lamar t-shirt over my head and he laid his head back on the couch. "I need to talk to you, but you ain't making this shit easy."

That slowed me down. What did he mean I wasn't making it easy? "What do you mean?"

"I need to tell you something that I know is gonna send you into panic mode and I hate seeing you that way."

I left his lap and sat beside him. "What is it?"

He seemed a little nervous now, but I was almost sure that it had nothing to do with us. "I went to the center, one day last week, to water and fertilize and heard some yelling."

"Serita and Sidney."

"Yeah. I wanted to let them know I was there, and I overheard what they were saying. I know what I had to say last time had come true, but it worked out for the best. So, I'm hoping this will, too."

It seemed like he was always in the right place at the right time. "Okay. So, what did you hear?"

"Sidney was telling Serita that they couldn't afford to keep you, if she went back. The center lost some of its funding when she left. So, one of y'all have to go or you would have to take a significant pay cut. Serita was doing her best to convince Sidney on why you have to stay. But Sidney wasn't hearing of it."

My heart rate sped up, but truthfully, I was expecting something like this to happen. Serita hadn't really been looking at the books as closely as she should have, before making those type of promises to me. But I assumed she would be getting donations from people she worked closely with. It was nothing for her to throw a fashion show and get some heavy hitters to donate big. But it seemed, when she left, she took their loyalty with her. "It's okay, baby. I'm not completely blind-sided. I've kind of been expecting this."

He exhaled, then pulled me in his arms. "So, what are you gonna do?"

"I don't know yet. I really don't want to work anywhere else, but I guess I better get my resume in order, huh?"

"Yeah, babe." He pulled me back on his lap. "Now, where were we?"

"That was it? That was all you wanted to talk about?"

"Well, I thought you would damn near break down, like last time, so I wanted to be prepared."

Grinding on him slowly, I slid my hand down his chest. "What if I wanted to break down on this dick?"

"Well, fuck. Break down on that shit, then."

I WAS TIRED AS HELL. I JUST KNEW AFTER I RODE ZAYSON'S ASS into the sunset, I was gonna get out of working out when we got to his house. That nigga said, "Naw. I don't care that you went buck wild on my shit. You still gon' put this time in."

I poked out my lip and tried to seduce his ass, but he wasn't having it. Especially since my last doctor's appointment, when he'd said I was borderline diabetic. Then, after my workout, he had the nerve to tell me that, after I soaked, I could do all the shit I was trying to do to skip my workout. He wasn't going to let me quit and I appreciated him for that. After my workouts, I always felt refreshed and my body was finally starting to get into the routine of it all. We worked out three days a week and once he finished breaking this horse, we would begin taking time to ride on Saturdays. I couldn't wait.

After he fucked the shit out of me, we ended up in the kitchen, with me wearing one of his shirts. "So, what are we cooking?"

"Honestly, I don't feel like cooking shit. You wanna go to Diamond S Diner?"

I scrunched my nose up. "Where's that?"

"Around the corner. Their food is good."

"Okay. If you say so. Let me get dressed."

I went to the back room and put on a maxi dress. Before I could leave the room, my phone rang. I looked at the caller ID to see J'Neka's name. I rolled my eyes. "Hello?"

"Hey, girl! So, we gon' turn up tonight or what?"

"Sorry, cuz. I'm with Zayson, this weekend. How about we plan something for next weekend?"

"Ugh! I guess I can forgive you, since that nigga fine and he feeling the hell out of you."

"Yes, he is, and I'm feeling the hell out of him."

"Aight. Don't renege on me for next weekend."

"I won't. Don't forget to call Kerry."

"I'm gonna call."

She ended the call and I immediately knew she was lying. J'Neka liked to party and fuck. Not only that, she liked a nigga that had shit going for himself. I didn't know how good Kerry was at faking the funk, but Neka could sniff out a bullshit ass dude like a hound dog. She was always fun to be around, when I didn't have a man. I watched her in action. It was more like I was her voice of reason, and made sure she got home safely, when she got drunk. To say she was so smart, she often made hasty ass decisions, signing a check that her ass couldn't cash.

Her daddy trusted me more than he trusted her, which was how I ended up always going places with her. He was my mother's brother. The two of them seemed a lot closer than Mom and Aunt Rose, though. Aunt Rose was the oldest, but Mom and Uncle George were closer in age. They seemed to get along better as well. I was almost sure there was a reason for that, but I hoped I never had to find out. I hated drama. While I knew whatever had happened might make me understand my mother better, I still didn't want to have to go through the process of knowing.

When I came out the room, Zayson was on the phone. "I told you we coming... don't you get your dick wet...? So, why you worrying about what I do...? Just because she yo' cousin don't mean you get to try to run me... Wait 'til I see yo' ass tomorrow. Them bulls ain't gon' have shit on me..."

He laughed loudly. There was no telling what Legend had said. When he said cousin and talked about bulls, I knew that was who he was talking to. "Man, that's my baby. You know, one day..." he stopped abruptly.

Zay turned around and saw me, then turned completely red. I wondered what he was about to say. He smiled, then went back to his call. "Nothing. Let me holla back. We about to get something to eat... aight."

I walked closer to him and wrapped my arms around his neck and kissed his lips as my stomach growled. His eyebrows rose, dramatically, as I laughed loudly and slapped his arm. "Come on, silly. I'm hungry as hell."

"Shit, you ain't gotta tell me. Yo' stomach already set that record straight."

When we got to the diner and ordered our food, we held hands while talking about my job and what my possibilities were. The only thing that made sense was to start looking for another job. Depending on how significant the pay cut would be would determine whether I stayed or not. Finally, he changed the subject, once we got our food. That grilled shrimp salad was calling out to me. I decided to eat healthy today, since we would deviate from my diet this weekend. "So, I decided I'm gonna start practicing with Red. I'd like you to meet his wife Shana and kind of bond with the ladies, since we'll be spending quite a bit of time with them."

"Okay. Are you excited?"

"Yeah. I hadn't been in a rodeo in years. After I bruised my ACL,

I knew I had to let it go. However, with team roping there's minimal risk."

"Well, I'm excited to see how all this works. I kind of know Harper, but what's Shana like?"

"Crazy as hell. She rodeos, too, though. Since she's been pregnant, she's been on a mini vacay. She's like seven months, I think."

"Well, I can't wait to meet her."

"You'll like her. I can't wait for you to see me in my element. That shit got me excited and nervous at the same time. Just my luck, I'll mess around and fuck up while you're watching."

I giggled at how excited he was to talk about it. That was an emotion Zayson didn't show too often. He was normally a happy person and he clowned around a lot, to garner a few laughs, but excitement was rare. Although we'd only been together about three weeks, I'd grown to know him more and more with each passing day. The only time I'd seen him really angry was with the situation with his brother. "I won't know the difference, Zay. So, relax. I can't wait to see you in action, though."

As he smiled at me, my eyes drifted to the door, where someone had entered the restaurant. The grin I wore faded. He could act an ass if he wanted to. Today, whether Zayson said something or not, he was gon' get a few words from me. I focused on my salad while Zay tore into his chicken fried steak. I was hoping Kerry's ass would just keep moving and not say shit. I wasn't so lucky. "What's up, Zay?"

Zayson looked up at his brother and hesitantly shook his outstretched hand. I supposed it was common for them to fight, then proceed like nothing ever happened. I continued eating my salad like I didn't see him. "How you doing?" he asked, his hand stretched out to me.

"I'm great. Thank you."

I was eating. So, I wasn't about to shake his hand. Not that I wanted to shake it anyway. Zayson smirked. I knew he was holding in his laughter. Kerry frowned slightly, then withdrew his hand. He wanted to call me a big bitch, but I could show him a big bitch. He'd better be glad he got any acknowledgement from me at all. I usually wasn't that petty, but he was going to apologize to me for what he knew I heard him say.

He walked away to be seated and Zay grabbed my hand. "I guess he got the hint."

"That wasn't a hint. He needs to apologize to you and me."

"He does, but he never apologizes. Mama said he went to their house the other day, like nothing ever happened."

"That's because y'all don't hold him accountable. I get that he's your brother, and their son, but somebody needs to knock his spoiled ass out."

"Don't worry. He's gonna get his sooner or later. Karma always bites him in the ass. Hard."

Whatever. Karma wasn't quick enough for me.

Chapter Sixteen

Zayson

"Shit! He hopped his ass right out of that damned rope."

"Naw. Yo' ass rusty. Yo' timing off. But that's what we practicing for. You gon' get it back," Legend said.

That's why I considered him and Red friends. They said what I needed to hear and didn't just go along with shit. That was how you knew when a muthafucka was trying to bring something to your life instead of just taking from it. "Yeah. You right. It's been a couple of years since I heeled a steer."

I glanced over at Kortlynn and she was talking to Harper and Shana. They seemed to be enjoying themselves. She looked back over at me and smiled, then blew me a kiss. I winked at her. That was my baby for real, and I knew, without a shadow of a doubt, that I loved her. "That's why yo' ass can't heel. You distracted. Do we need to ask the women to go in the house?" Red asked.

"Naw. I got it this time."

"Uh huh. You betta, nigga."

I laughed at the smirk on his face. That was their way of pushing me to do better. They did this shit almost every day, so they knew it would take me a minute to get in the groove. Legend got the steer ready while I backed my horse in the box on the right side of the steer and Red backed up on its left side. When Legend released him, the steer would run up the middle, and Red would rope the horns and take a dally, which was wrapping the rope around the saddle horn, and turn left, causing the steer to turn left as well. It was my job to rope his hind legs.

Like Legend had said, my timing was off. I had to throw the rope at exactly the right time, or the steer could hop right out of it before it could tighten around his legs or I could just miss him altogether. I could see the ladies watching us, but I closed my eyes for a second, so I could focus. This time, I had to heel that fucker, even if only to prove to myself that I could still do this shit and be good at it. Looking over at Red and Legend, Red gave the head nod. Once the steer broke for it, our barriers dropped, and we went after it. Red did his job, perfectly, and I threw my rope and caught that son of a bitch.

It was about damn time. The ladies were all clapping and cheering. I looked over to see my baby standing on her feet with an excited expression on her face. Knowing I had her support was like the wind in a nigga sail. After that, I didn't miss another one. "Well, looka here. A nigga back in the saddle," Legend said.

We all laughed. When I dismounted the horse, and had left the gate, Kortlynn ran to me and hugged me tightly. "You did so good!"

"Thank you, baby," I said, then chuckled.

Legend and Red were behind me, laughing and cracking jokes, I was sure. "Harper! I didn't see yo' ass running to me to say I did a good job."

"I'm gon' run to yo' ass later, Legend."

Red walked over to Shana and put his hand on her stomach.

Looking back at my baby, I asked, "You wanna come home, with me, and take a shower? We'll come back to eat."

"I wanna take a shower alright."

Not that she didn't already have hips, but as much as we had been getting it in, I could notice the difference in them. Not to mention, her stamina had gotten better from working out and she'd lost five pounds in two weeks. "Mmm hmm. My freak. Let's go."

"Yo! Where y'all going?" Red yelled.

"I'm going take a shower! We'll be back!" I yelled back.

Red twisted his mouth to the side, as I chuckled, then looked down at my baby. "You ready?"

"Beyond ready."

AFTER WE'D GOTTEN IT IN, WHILE IN THE SHOWER, I WAS READY to suck on that thang between her legs, when her phone rang. She didn't want to answer it, but when she saw it was Serita, she answered it, on speakerphone, quickly. "Hello?"

"Hi, Kortlynn. How's your weekend going?"

"It's going great. How about yours?"

"Shitty."

"Why?"

"Because I have something horrible to tell you and I can't even have a drink to calm my nerves. I know what I promised you, but Sidney informed me of the center's financial state. Unless I can get Shawn and Sonya to make a substantial donation, I'm gonna have to let you go."

Kortlynn closed her eyes briefly. At least I'd warned her. "I'm so sorry, Kortlynn. I really am. I can almost guarantee Sonya won't donate. So, unless Shawn goes behind her back, that's the only way I'll get money. He's already given me half a million to pay off debts and to start fresh. While he has plenty of money, that doesn't mean he has to give any to me. So, I'm blessed to have gotten that out of him."

"I understand. How much time do I have?"

"A month, maybe. God, I'm so sorry," she sobbed.

I rubbed Kortlynn's back, as she tried to keep a poker face. Working at that center meant everything to her. She was looking forward to the start of the summer program, in the next two weeks. Now, she would only be there for a week or two of it, if that. Listening to her excitement when she spoke of those girls and the programs she had lined up for the summer, made me proud of just how passionate she was. Now, due to no fault of her own, that may all be taken from her. That was why I was determined to work for myself. Someone else having the power to say whether you had a job or not was too much stress for anybody. Non-profits were even harder, because if they lost funding, for any reason, shit like this could happen.

"Serita, it's okay. Don't cry."

"I can only afford to offer you a position that pays half your salary. But again, pray that Shawn will make a donation."

"I will. I'll see you, Monday."

When she ended the call, she swallowed hard, as I stared at her, waiting for her to break down. That didn't happen, though. "Well, there's that."

She stood from the bed and dropped her phone in her purse, then came back to the bed. After laying down, she spread her legs. "I really need some tender loving right now. You think you can give me that?"

"Anything you need, baby. I got'chu."

I was about to put my face between her legs, but she pulled me. "I need to feel you, now, Zayson. Please."

I didn't waste any time sliding right in, trying to love her pain away. Slowly, I stroked her, causing the emotions to fill my heart. Looking at her, as I debated on whether I should tell her now, I decided against it. She was already feeling emotional. If she wasn't in love with me, then my admission would make her feel worse. She lifted her hips and gave me more of her. It felt like we were levitating in the feelings we had for one another... the love I had for her. My lips landed on hers and she moaned softly.

I wanted her to feel every emotion I was feeling. She was so independent, so I knew she wouldn't ask for help. I was going to have to help her find work that she would be happy with, until Serita got her shit together. Pulling away from her lips, I left a trail of kisses from her neck to her hard nipples. They were begging for my attention and the moment my tongue circled around them and my lips encompassed them, Kortlynn came. "Zaaaayy, yes, baby."

I groaned, as I felt the extra warmth between her legs. My dick wanted to get excited and pick up the pace, but I had to hold the reins back, until my baby said she needed more. She arched her back and moaned loudly, as a tear slid down her cheek. Wiping it away with my thumb, I then kissed that spot. "Damn, baby," I said in her ear, as I hooked her leg in the crook of my arm.

The head of my dick was gently pushing into her cervix, as she panted. She pushed me off her, causing me to roll to my back, then she mounted me. Closing her eyes, she began rocking on my dick, giving me that gushy shit. Biting my bottom lip and grabbing her hips, I watched her sex faces, noticing how much she was enjoying it. She always did, but today was different. She was sensitive and in her feelings. When she opened her eyes, she stared into mine. "Zayson?"

"Yeah, baby?"

"I need you so much."

"And you got me, baby. All of me."

"Good, because... oh, God... you have all of me. Zaysoooon... shit."

She was cumming again and, while I wanted to fuck up the way she walked, I laid there and let her have her moment, while slowly winding the dick into her. Her soft moans were filled with passion and they affected me just as much as her screams did, if not more. Resting her hands on my chest, she began circling her hips, first clockwise, then counterclockwise. I dropped my head back, because I didn't know how much longer I would last. My shit was hard as a damn sugar cane pole and it was ready to extract that creamy goodness right to her womb. "Fuuuck, girl."

"Don't cum, yet, Zay. I have more to... say."

She wanted me to perform a damn miracle, if she didn't want me to cum, with the way she was riding a nigga. I knew she felt I was close. She sat up, then lifted herself off it. It was glistening in her juices and I couldn't help but lick my lips. I'd wanted to taste her so bad. "Zay? I hope what I say don't make you leave me, but I'm willing to risk it, because I can't keep this shit to myself any longer."

My dick was starting to deflate. I didn't know what she had to tell me, but I was nervous as shit now. "No, he needs to stay awake for this."

She lowered her head and sucked that nigga back to life. I grabbed her by the hair. "Man, please just say the shit. You torturing me, girl."

She released my dick, giving me the satisfaction of the popping noise and allowing the spit to fall from her mouth. I took a deep breath, as my eyes rolled to the back of my head. My shit was throbbing, needing to nut like never before. "Zay, I love you."

My eyes popped open. For some reason, I wasn't expecting her to say that. Did she really feel that way or was she just vulnerable because she might lose her job? I pulled her to me, then rolled her over to her back. Laying atop her beautiful body, I slid down her torso. "How long you been loving me, Kort?"

I began indulging in the sight before my eyes, waiting for her to answer my question. "At least a week. How do you feel about me?"

I continued sucking on her clit, and inserted my fingers inside of her, caressing her g-spot until she came. Sliding inside of her, I looked in her eyes. "I love you, too, girl. I've felt that way for a while, but I didn't want to scare you away because it was so soon."

"Zay... shit. You can fuck me now. Shit! Fuck me baby!"

"You ain't gotta tell me twice."

I pounded her shit immediately, then picked her legs up, as my phone rang. That shit was gon' have to wait, because this pussy didn't deserve to be put on hold. Before long, I was sweating and grunting. "Kortlynn, shit, baby. I love you."

"I love you, too, Zay."

It felt so good to let that shit out, but to hear her say it to me felt even better. I kissed her thick lips, then released the inevitable, the shit that had been begging to be free. Lowering my forehead to hers, I shuddered at the feeling I got every time we fucked... every time we made love. It was stronger, now, though, because there was nothing left to say.

When we disconnected, my phone was ringing again. I rolled my eyes and went to it to see Legend's number. "Yeah?"

"Get the fuck off my cousin and come eat, nigga. The food getting cold and we 'bout to demolish this shit without y'all."

"Nigga, go to hell. We'll be there in a lil bit." I ended the call, then looked at Kortlynn as she giggled. "I ain't gotta tell you who that was."

"Red or Legend for sure."

"Your blocking-ass cousin."

I helped her up from the bed, then held her in my arms. "So, this is what it feels like to be in love. Makes me think, all the other times, I was only infatuated."

"I know what'chu mean, baby girl. Damn, I know what'chu mean." After kissing her lips, I continued, "Let's get dressed so I don't have to fuck your cousin up."

Chapter Seventeen

K ortlynn

DESPITE THE FACT THAT I COULD BE LOSING MY JOB, WE HAD AN amazing time yesterday. I knew Zayson was in love with me. Whenever he looked at me, I could feel it. And the way his body communicated with mine, there was no way he didn't love me. Of course, we had to hear all the shit talking from Legend and Red, once we got back to Red's house. I didn't care, since I got to eat some fried chicken, red beans and rice with sausage, cornbread and greens. I tuned their asses right out and enjoyed dinner.

Harper, Shana and I gelled ridiculously well. It was like we'd known one another for years. As we watched the guys practice, we laughed at how much they were alike. They all had tempers, at times, loved sex and were as country as a suga sammich. That was how Shana had said it, and Harper and I couldn't help but laugh, as we looked at the three of them, out there, wearing their cowboy boots and Cinch jeans. Zayson's temper wasn't as bad as Red and Legend's, but it was there. He didn't waste any time laying his brother out that day.

But, watching him in action, riding that horse and swinging a rope was sexy as hell. I was in a damn trance for his first couple of attempts. I hadn't even noticed he'd missed the steer. Hell, when he roped it the first time, Harper had to nudge me. I was so caught up in how his dick and ass looked in those jeans, I could barely pay attention to anything else. However, after I missed the first time, even though I'd jumped from my seat clapping, like I'd seen the whole thing, I paid complete attention to the next round.

As we sat at Zayson's parents' house, all I wanted to do was go to sleep. I knew Zay could see that damn monkey having a field day on my back. Mrs. Barbara and I had already cleaned the kitchen and Zay and Mr. Henry were watching a basketball game. When the door opened, I woke all the way up. I knew it could only be one person just walking in the house. After slightly rolling my eyes, Zay stood to his feet and held his hand out to help me from my seat. Placing my hand in his and standing, his brother walked around the corner. A slow smile made its way to his lips. "Hey, Daddy... Mama... Zay."

He looked at me and turned the other way. "We're gonna go, y'all. Dinner was delicious, Ma."

"Kerry, don't be disrespectful. I know you've met Kortlynn," Mrs. Barbara said.

Aww, shit. "Well, the last time I spoke to her, she didn't respond."

"You're a liar." I didn't give Zayson a chance to open his mouth. "I spoke back to you, but I refused to shake your hand. I was eating and I didn't know where your hands had been."

"Seem like every time I see you, you're eating. I definitely know you ate here."

Before I could come back, Zay snatched his ass up. "The last time you disrespected my woman, I thought I set you straight."

Mrs. Barbara and Mr. Henry sprang to their feet, trying to get

Zayson to let Kerry go. I made my way past them and wrapped my arms around Zay. "Baby, he's not worth it. Come on."

Zayson's grip on Kerry loosened, as his lip twitched. I was afraid he was going to do something he would regret. Zay backed away from Kerry, not taking his eyes off him as Kerry smirked and glanced at me. When we got to the kitchen, Zay grabbed my hand, spun me around and practically drug me out of his parents' house. "Zay, please, slow down. My legs aren't as long as yours."

He stopped, then turned to look at me, as his mama approached. "You shouldn't be subjected to his behavior. I'm sorry, baby. And I'm embarrassed."

I slid my hand up his cheek. "You have no reason to be embarrassed. I just won't come when he's here. I'm sorry I snapped. I can usually control my temper but, for some reason, your brother tap dances on all my nerve endings."

"You didn't snap. You were just speaking up for yourself and I don't have a problem with that. Fuck him. You can come to my parents' house whenever you want. He needs to call to see if he can come over."

"I'm so sorry, Kortlynn."

We both turned to see Mrs. Barbara. She hugged me, then looked at a still angry Zay. "Son, I apologize."

"Mama, I'm so sick of his shit. This is the woman I love. If he can't respect that shit, then I will buss his ass every time he open his mouth."

Her eyebrows had risen, then she looked at me. "Y'all are in love?"

"I love your son to death, Mrs. Barbara."

She wrapped her arms around us. "I'm gon' take care of his ass. Kortlynn, you are always welcome at my house. I'll put his ass out first. I love you, daughter-in-law."

I giggled, because I could remember when she told me I would be her daughter-in-law, almost a month ago. "I love you, too."

Zayson kissed his mama, then opened the car door for me. When he joined me inside, he looked like he wanted to spit nails. I drove to his house and he got out, then walked around to my side. Usually, on Sundays, I would drop him off and head home, but I couldn't leave with him like this. We couldn't end our weekend together like this. He looked shocked when I got out the car. "Baby, we can't let him win. We can't give him the power. He had that smirk on his face because he succeeded in getting us all worked up over his own ignorance."

Zay grabbed my hand and led me in the house. "You right, baby," he said, as he led me to the couch.

When he sat, I was about to sit next to him, but he pulled me in his lap. "I love your positivity and how you can calm me down. I'd already planned to be waiting at that fucker's house when you left. But, you right. He don't deserve our energy. He's insecure with who he is, as a man, and tries to attack other people because of that."

"Exactly. You just focus on your upcoming rodeo career and taking our relationship to an even more powerful level. We complement one another so well."

"That we do."

We sat in the quietness, embracing one another, until I ended up naked, all over again, and sitting on his dick.

⚜

"Daddy, you look really good."

"Thanks, baby girl. You ain't gon' believe this."

"What?"

"Mary Hebert brought her uppity ass to my house to see how I was doing."

"Shut the hell up! Daddy, you lying!"

"If I'm lying, I'm flying."

"I haven't really been talking to her since she disrespected Zayson."

"Well, maybe I should stop talking to you, since I hadn't even met him yet."

"I'm sorry, Daddy. I'll bring him by, one day, for lunch. But I still can't believe Mom came to see you. What did she say?"

"That she was sorry I was going through this and she wished she wouldn't have been so stubborn. She's going to start coming with me on Mondays."

I almost gave him an "aww" and felt proud of my mother, then I thought about it. Daddy had plenty of money. That was what she was after. Looking at him, I knew I couldn't keep what I was feeling from showing through my facial expressions. "What is it, Kortlynn?"

"Be careful with Mom. You know how she is. She always has a hidden agenda."

"You forgot? I knew her before you did. Ain't shit changed about Mary. She after my money. I'm no fool."

"I'm glad you peeping game."

"Mary ain't got no game. I'm letting her think that."

I chuckled as I sat next to him. It was Thursday and we were at the treatment facility. They were just getting started. We spent our morning talking about Zayson and my job that would be ending soon. He told me not to worry about a thing. I knew if I had no one else, Zayson and my daddy would be there for me, so worry was the last thing I was doing. Serita had avoided me all week, like she was scared I was gonna attack her or something. I knew that was probably more out of embarrassment. However, I was going to ask her, either tomorrow or Monday, if she'd talked to her ex-husband. She had huge anxiety issues, even before the drug use. She'd told me that she grew up in state custody, her entire life, and that was why she had such a passion for helping girls.

While some people had it okay, in foster homes, she suffered a tremendous amount of abuse. They weren't as thorough, back then, as they are now, with checking the children's welfare. If the child said they were okay, then they left it at that. Besides checking iron levels, there wasn't much else they checked internally. So, her mental state was already fragile. It didn't help that she pushed Shawn away. He seemed to be the only one that could help her by calming her down.

Whatever the case, I needed her to appeal to him, on behalf of my job, so I knew where to go from here. I wasn't the type that liked to depend on anyone else. If I had to, then I wouldn't shy away from it but, at that point, all my other options had to be exhausted. I'd already applied for several state jobs, but I knew my heart wouldn't be there, like it was working at Integrity.

Looking over at my daddy, I could tell he was tired. This shit had to be hard on his body. Gently rubbing his bald head, I asked softly, "You okay?"

"Yeah. Three more hours," he whispered.

A text came through, on my phone, and I knew it was Zayson with lunch. Glancing at my phone to confirm, I looked back at my dad. "Today isn't a good day to meet Zayson, huh?"

"Any day is a good day to meet the man that stole my baby's heart."

I watched him perk up, then briefly closed my eyes. He always gave me what I wanted. "Daddy, he knows why we're here. You don't have to pretend that all is well."

"Go get the man from outside, baby girl."

I smiled at him, then went outside to meet Zay. He was standing there, looking sexy as ever, in his jeans, turquoise shirt and matching tennis shoes. This man made me weak at every turn and I knew I did the same for him. "Hey, baby."

He kissed my lips, then smiled and said, "Hey. You look gorgeous."

"Thank you. And thanks for lunch." I took the bag from him and inhaled the scent of the grilled chicken wrap. "You wanna come in for a moment?"

"Umm... sure. Let me park."

He'd always pulled under the awning, since he wouldn't be staying. I could tell he was shocked that I'd asked him to come in. Once he rejoined me, we walked inside, hand in hand. Once we got to my daddy, he smiled. "Kort, I knew you liked them tall, but damn."

We all laughed, as he extended his hand to Zayson. I made the introductions and Zay sat in my chair, then pulled me on his lap. Daddy already knew how we'd met, so he engaged Zay in conversation about horses and rodeoing. They were getting along perfectly, like I'd gotten along with his parents, until Mary walked in. *Why in the hell was she here?* She knew Thursdays I would be with Dad. I stood from Zayson's lap, and he stood as well. After shaking my dad's hand, he kissed my cheek. "I'm gonna go, baby."

"Okay. I'll see you later?"

"Most definitely. I love you."

"I love you, too, Zay."

"You don't have to leave. I won't be here long, Kortlynn."

"Zayson is leaving. I'm not leaving my daddy until I bring him home."

She glanced over at Zayson, as I grabbed his hand. It finally dawned on me. She was jealous of our relationship. I had a man that loved me unconditionally and she had no one. It was something she'd never had, because her hunger for material things always got in the way. She spent most of her time trying to trap a man that didn't want her, instead of focusing on the one that did. Aunt Rose had told me of a man that was in love with her, around the same time she was fooling around with my daddy.

I walked Zayson out but, when we got to his truck, I didn't want to let him go. "You okay, baby?"

"Yeah. I just think I'm feeling a little sensitive. Daddy's in a lot of pain, although he's trying to hide it. I also just realized that my mama is jealous of our relationship. I think that she thought, because of my weight, I'd be alone like her. It's done something to her backwards ass ego that I have a man and she doesn't."

"Well, I know seeing your dad go through this is hard for you. Seeing a parent go through pain isn't easy. However, the situation with your mom, let that roll off your back. You can't sacrifice your happiness for hers."

"I know, baby. And I'm not willing to, either."

"Good. So, you gon' come stay with me tonight? I can fuck all that sensitivity away."

"Really?" I asked, while rolling my eyes.

"Shiiiid, I can love it away, too. Whatever you want. You got that from me."

He pulled me in his arms and kissed my forehead. "I want it all, big daddy."

"Big daddy, huh? You gon' get all this shit, right here, outside. Keep on. You like teasing a nigga."

I giggled, as I ran my hand down his cheek. "Why you always gotta say nasty shit?"

I was waiting for him to say what Ray said in the movie *Life*. We said it at least every other day, because Zay was always saying or doing something nasty. I loved every minute of it, though.

Refusing to let me down, he said, "'Cause I'm a nasty muthafucka!" He laughed for a minute. "The fuck you thought, girl?"

I laughed and hugged him tightly. "I'll be there when I leave Daddy's house. I better get back in there to see what poison Mary is trying to unleash on him. I love you, baby."

"Aight. I love you, too. I got some shit planned for us."

"Ooooh. I like surprises, so I can't wait."

I kissed his lips, then forced myself to let him go and headed back inside. As I walked to where my daddy was, my mama was still sitting there, and looked me from head to toe, as I approached. She was about to be on her bullshit. I sat on the other side of Daddy and he grabbed my hand. "Zayson is a nice young man. I'm glad you're happy, baby girl."

"Yeah. And you've lost weight. Is he forcing you to work out?"

"Daddy, close your ears."

He put his hands over his ears, as I decided to tell my mama the real. "He's not forcing me to do anything. I chose to start working out to build my stamina. I need to be able to keep up with him, in the bedroom, when he's making passionate love to me without getting tired."

Her face was as red as the flames of hell. I was tickled and, to put the icing on the cake, I crossed my legs, something I'd never really been able to do comfortably. Daddy pulled his hands from his ears and glanced back and forth from me to my mother. "Is it safe?"

I couldn't help but laugh, because I knew he'd heard every word. "Yes. I'm about to leave before your daughter decides to divulge any more of her sex life."

I slowly shook my head. She asked for it. Leaning over, she kissed Daddy's cheek. I couldn't help but slightly roll my eyes. She was so damn fake and everyone around her knew it.

Chapter Eighteen

✿❦✿

Z ayson

WHEN KORTLYNN WAS GONNA GET HERE AND SEE THESE HORSES saddled, she was gon' have a fit. I'd been promising her that we would ride, and I would show her some things. She'd never ridden before and she was ready to experience how peaceful it could be. Whenever I needed to think heavily about something, I'd go for a ride. Also, when my daddy was sick, going through his blockage issues, it helped me ease my mind. Daddy was so close to a massive heart attack, had he not gone to the hospital, when he did, we would've been planning his funeral.

I could definitely understand the sensitivity my baby was feeling about her dad, because I'd been there. Now, that bullshit with her mom, I couldn't understand. How in the fuck could you be jealous of your own kid? That was some evil and childish shit, if I ever seen it. And the way Mrs. Semien talked to her, when we went to dinner there, let me know it was more to that shit that not even Kortlynn knew.

As I brushed Daisy's mane, Kortlynn pulled in the driveway. I smiled and made my way to her car, anxious to witness her excitement about the horses being saddled. When she got out, I could tell she'd been crying. That was something I rarely saw her do. Even though she was sensitive, at times, it was like she was taught to keep her tears to herself. When we met, I pulled her in my arms. "You aight, baby?"

"I'm okay, Zay." She looked around me, toward the horses. "Are we riding today?"

"Mmm hmm."

She started clapping and got a lil pep in her step, as we continued walking. "I'm just a little worried about my daddy. He was so weak, when I brought him home. For a moment, I didn't know how I would get him in the house."

"I'm so sorry, baby. You know I have a flexible schedule, so if you need me, I can be there on Thursdays."

"Zay! You would do that for me?"

"Girl, I'd do anything for you."

I watched a tear trickle down her cheek, and she quickly swiped it away. "Daddy talked about you almost the whole time, after you left."

"Hopefully, good things."

I stopped her from walking by standing in front of her. "You talk about your daddy hiding his pain, but it seems like that's what you're trying to do now. It's okay for you to let that shit go with me."

"I'm okay, Zay. Really. I've never really been a crier. My heart is heavy, though."

I slid my hand in hers, then led her to the horses. "Well, you'll get to see what I'm talking about when you get past the initial shock of being on a horse. I'm glad you have on pants."

"Me, too."

I slid my hands around her waist and had her put her left foot in the stirrup, so she could swing her right leg over. I had to help her lift herself a little, but all that working out was paying off. "Good, baby. You feel okay up there?" I asked, as I handed her the reins.

"Yeah. I feel okay. Just a little nervous."

"Relax. I'm gonna walk him around, for a second, before we ride out."

"Okay."

After pulling my boots on, I grabbed the reins from her and walked them around the pasture. The breeze blew through her hair and I could see her eyes close for a moment. When Jack whinnied, her eyes popped open. I couldn't help but chuckle. She had a tight ass grip on the saddle horn. "Relax, baby. He can feel your nerves. Rub his neck and let him know you at ease with him. You know how you get a lil groove in your hips when you first start riding this horse? Do the same with him."

She rolled her eyes. "Must everything be about sex?"

"Hell, yeah. Have you looked in the mirror? You sexy as hell, girl. My horse be begging to get saddled every time you near."

She blushed and gently rubbed Jack. "What's his name?"

"Jack."

I continued walking and she started talking to him. Smiling at how comfortable she was getting, I made my way back to Daisy, so I could ride with her. "Zay?"

"Yeah?"

"Tomorrow, I'm supposed to be going out with J'Neka. So, I won't get to you until Saturday."

"Aight. I'll come get you for lunch and kick it with you until y'all leave, if that's cool."

"You being in my space is always cool."

I handed her the reins, then got on my horse. After getting situated, I told her how to make Jack go. Although, I had these horses so well-trained, they listened to whatever I told them to do. Kicks were never really necessary, but I wanted her to learn, in case she was ever on someone else's horse. She kicked Jack so tenderly, he didn't move. "Babe, you can't be scared. Put a little umph in it."

She kicked him harder and he started walking. The smile that brightened her face made me smile as well. We rode and talked while I showed her what to do. I could see her relax more and more, as we rode. We talked about her dad and briefly about her mom, before coming back to the pin. I'd even asked her why it took so long for her to meet her dad and she'd revealed to me that he didn't want kids and that Mrs. Semien told her that her mama was trying to trap him. That was some crazy shit if I ever heard of it. But I think it also explained why her mama didn't want her with me. She didn't think I could take care of Kortlynn financially. That was what was important to her. Somehow, Kortlynn had learned how to navigate through life on her own.

Once her and her dad connected, and had gotten comfortable with one another, it was like he'd been there the whole time, she'd said. After our ride, we went inside and showered together and, of course, engaged in activities that made me a nasty muthafucka.

❦

"Baby girl, I'm at yo' place. You still at work?"

"Yeah. I'm running a little behind. There's a key in the planter by the door. Go on in."

"Aight. See you when you get here."

"Okay. Love you."

"Love you, too."

It was rare that Kortlynn had to work late but, since Serita had been back, they'd been working overtime to get their summer program off the ground. We'd had an amazing evening yesterday and an even better lunch today. With each passing day, Kortlynn and I were getting closer than close. She was going out with her cousin, tonight, but tomorrow we were going out to Pappadeaux's with

Legend, Harper, Red and Shana. Kortlynn had really enjoyed their company last weekend.

As I sat there, I let out a huge yawn. It had been a long day, but I couldn't end it without seeing my baby. I'd worked the colt a bit, this morning, to make sure he was ready to be returned to his owner. He didn't let me down. I was awake long before Kortlynn had left this morning. After feeding the horses, I'd had to mow the field with the tractor and, this weekend, I would be mowing the hay field as well. Just thinking about all the work ahead of me, this weekend, caused me to doze off.

Before I could get into a deep sleep, I heard the door open. I stood to my feet and headed to the door to greet baby girl, only to run into J'Neka. "Hey! Sorry. You probably thought I was Kortlynn. She told me she would be home, in a little bit, so I came over thinking we'd get here at the same time. When I turned the doorknob, it was unlocked, so I came on in."

"Oh, okay."

I didn't have a good feeling about this shit but, if Kortlynn was on her way, I couldn't trip. She was just right down the street. I sat back on the couch and J'Neka said she was going in the room to put her and Kortlynn's outfits together. I gave her a head nod and laid my head back on the couch. The nap I was starting when J'Neka had arrived was about to be everything, so I wasn't finna let that shit get away from me.

Nigga wake up and look at your baby. I was sleeping so good, I couldn't seem to wake up. Kortlynn was kissing all over me and was about to give me that neck action. My hand slid over her head trying to grip her hair, but that shit woke me all the way up. Kortlynn didn't have short hair. My eyes opened to see her cousin on her knees in front of me, stroking my dick. "Yo! Hell naw! What the fuck you on?!"

"You know you want this shit. Ain't no way you feeling Kortlynn like you pretending to be."

I jumped up from the sofa, trying to get my hard dick back in my pants and hold this bitch off me at the same time, as Kortlynn walked through the door. She dropped her purse and keys to the floor. Man, I couldn't believe I was in this predicament. I only saw shit like this on TV. "Kort, I swear this ain't what it look like. I'd dozed off and woke up to her stroking my dick. I promise you, I don't want her."

"Shut the fuck up, Zay."

Her eyes were on J'Neka. She'd never looked at me. "Kortlynn, you actually believe him? He was flirting with me and trying to get at me. He even went as far as taking his dick out to ask me if I thought I could handle it."

"You lying ass bitch!" I yelled, right before Kortlynn punched her in her shit.

Oh, fuck! She laid J'Neka's ass out and had straddled her and was beating the shit out of her. I almost didn't want to intervene, because she deserved that beat down. I pulled her off J'Neka and she glared at me like she thought I was guilty of something. *What the fuck?* J'Neka stood from the floor. "So, I guess you gon' believe him, huh? The typical desperate female. Go after the woman and let the man off the hook."

"What goes on between me and Zay is none of your fucking business. Now, get the fuck out of my place before I jump on your ass again. Don't bring yo' hoe ass back over here. Act like I don't exist. I knew you did some ratchet shit, sometimes, but I didn't think you were crazy enough to do that shit to me."

J'Neka was still standing there like she didn't know what to do, until Kortlynn screamed, "Get the fuck out!"

Once the door slammed, her attention turned to me. I lifted my hands in the air. "Kort, baby, I was asleep, for real. I never approached her."

"Zay, you got to be a fucking idiot."

"What? You think I want her?"

"No. You know I trust you with everything in me. I know her ratchet ass and have been knowing her my whole life. So, I know what kind of fucked up shit she's capable of. However, I'm still tryna figure out why in the fuck y'all were in my place alone."

"Baby, I didn't lock the door. She walked in."

"And why in the fuck you didn't walk out?"

"Man, you gotta be bullshitting me. I ain't do shit, and you still fucking mad at me?"

"You shouldn't have been in here alone with her, Zay! How hard is that concept to understand? If you don't get why I'm angry at you, then you can get the fuck out, too!"

I was so fucking angry, I snatched my keys from the countertop and walked the hell out. For her to say I played a part in this irritated the fuck out of me. When I got to my truck, I got in and slammed the door. My temper was getting the best of me, so I started the truck and took a minute to calm down. I laid my head back against the seat and closed my eyes. After taking a few deep breaths, I backed out and headed home.

However, by the time I got to China, I understood her point. I sat in my driveway, thinking about the feeling I had the moment I saw J'Neka. I knew it was a bad idea for us to be alone but, when she said Kortlynn was on her way, I figured she didn't have time to be conniving. Kortlynn only worked like five minutes away. I should've known that bitch was probably lying. Now, I'd incited an argument between me and my baby. Immediately grabbing my phone, I called her to try to make it right, but she didn't answer. So, I did the next best thing. I backed out my driveway and headed back to Beaumont.

Chapter Nineteen

K ortlynn

FEELING ANGER IN MY HEART TOWARD ONE OF THE PEOPLE I loved the most was killing me. I couldn't stop pacing. When I walked in my place and saw him trying to stuff his hard dick back in his pants, I felt so betrayed... by both of them. J'Neka had always been a trifling hoe, but she was my cousin. She'd never crossed me. We always talked about her changing her ways and, when she went to Denton, she claimed she'd gotten a fresh start and was working on herself. I believed her. I still wouldn't have trusted her around my man, but I believed that she was trying to do better.

I could see he was clearly trying to push her away and I knew, in my heart, that Zayson wouldn't betray me that way. But his dick was rock hard, and that shit was unnerving. It wasn't wet or anything, so her touch had him that way. I knew dicks had minds of their own, but that didn't stop me from feeling a certain way about it. Then, the bitch had the nerve to lie on him. When she said Zay approached her, that was it.

For her to lie about it, so blatantly, let me know that Zay was innocent in the matter. She attacked his character and that was just as bad as what she was trying to do when I walked in. Anger had consumed me, and it was a miracle she was able to walk out of my apartment. Had Zayson not pulled me off her, she probably wouldn't have.

I finally went to my bedroom and laid on the bed. Not knowing how to proceed with Zayson was bothering the hell out of me. He was so angry, and I couldn't, for the life of me, understand why. I clearly stated that the reason I was angry at him was because he was in my place with her, alone. The minute she walked in, he should've said, *you know, I better wait in my truck for Kortlynn.* The shit just didn't look right. Shouldn't he have abstained from the very appearance of evil?

Had he done that, I wouldn't have walked in on what I did. She wouldn't have had the opportunity to do the shit that she did. This was a whole mess and I silently prayed that Zayson and I could move on from this and accept it as a lesson learned. Regardless of blood, I should've refused to hang around J'Neka. We were grown and there was no reason for me to be around her, watching to make sure she made it home safely. That was some high school shit that I should have let go of a long time ago.

I snapped on Zay. I shouldn't have called him an idiot. It was honestly a poor judgement call... a bad decision to stay there with her. He had to know what I was dealing with, walking in and seeing everything I saw. That was so hard. It was like I had flashbacks of all my failed relationships, in that moment, even though I knew that Zayson was only guilty of being there alone with her. As I laid in the bed, replaying everything that happened in my mind, over and over again, there was a knock at the door.

I chose to ignore it, as I tried to think of ways I could have better handled things with Zayson. Letting anger consume me, the way I had, was dangerous and Zayson deserved a calm and level-headed explanation of why I got angry. Running my hand down my face, I, again, heard the knock at the door. If it was that bitch, I was just gonna get mad all over again. I got up from the bed and practically stomped to the door. Looking through the peephole, my breath got caught in my throat. It was Zayson. Why was he back? As I opened the door, my heart started running a race that I had a hard time keeping up with. His face was red. "Can I come in?"

I nodded and stepped aside, allowing him to walk past me. When I closed the door, he was still standing there, waiting for me. Grabbing my hand, he led me to the couch. As I was about to sit next to him, he pulled me to his lap. That eased the tension in my soul, because I was expecting the worst. "Baby, I'm sorry. I get what you were saying. I just had to think about it for a minute. Please forgive me."

I hugged his neck and kissed his cheek. "I'm sorry, too, for yelling and calling you an idiot."

"Damn. You did call me an idiot. A *fucking* idiot."

The smirk on his lips let me know that everything was alright in our world, but I needed to know how it got to what I saw. "Zay, how did it get so far?"

"You ever been asleep, but couldn't seem to wake yourself up? It was like that... like I was dreaming, and it was you kissing me. She was about to go down on me and, when I grabbed her hair, my eyes popped open. Before she could put her lips on it, I got up so quick, I almost fell."

I nodded my head, then laid on his shoulder. He wrapped his arms around my waist and kissed my forehead. "When I started thinking about how you felt, I imagined if I had walked in my house to something similar between you and my brother. I would have had a fucking fit. It seems like our love is a misunderstanding to people. But that's cool. We're the only ones that need to understand it."

He was so right about that shit. I didn't have a problem blocking every damn body out of my life that couldn't respect our love. Lifting my head, I put my lips to his and that was it. He stood from his seat, still holding me in his arms. This nigga was strong as an ox, because baby girl was still a good two-twenty. Walking to the kitchen, he sat me on the island and began pulling off my pants. "Baby, in the kitchen?"

"Hell, yeah, 'cause I'm 'bout to eat. Any objections?"

"Oh, shit! Handle your business, baby."

"I don't think you ready."

I couldn't respond, as I laid on the countertop of the island, wondering what he was doing. He went to my refrigerator and stood there for a minute. My curiosity was piqued, because I couldn't see what he was grabbing. However, the moment he turned around, I got excited. In his hands were whipped cream, chocolate syrup, caramel and cherries. "As soon as I put all these toppings on this pussy, then you'll be ready. I'm gon' eat the fuck out of this Cream Sundae."

He licked his lips, then took his time dressing my shit just so he could eat it off. When his head went to my Sundae, I shivered in anticipation. Putting my hands on either side of his head, I closed my eyes and enjoyed the feel of his tongue on my flesh. I could imagine that he was making a mess. The slurping noises he was making, and the moans of total satisfaction coming from him, turned me on even more so. Opening my eyes, as he came up, just as I imagined, he had whipped cream, chocolate and caramel from his nose to his chin. "Come, taste this shit, Kort."

As if I were electrocuted by the countertop, I sat up and immediately began licking and sucking on his face. He grabbed my face and plunged his tongue in my mouth. I felt like I wanted to cum. My clit felt like it was rubbing the damned countertop. Zayson gently pushed me back to the countertop and went down to my Sundae. "Damn, it's melting. Let me get to it."

He went in for the kill and I screamed to the high heavens. My shit squirted like a water fountain and Zayson couldn't be more pleased with himself. The smirk on his lips, as he pushed his fingers inside of me, making that fountain even higher, told me that he was amused. When it stopped, he sat me up, removing my shirt and bra, then undressed himself. Pulling my nipples in his mouth simultaneously, threatened to do more damage. My fingernails raked his back, as I could feel myself about to cum again. He lifted his head. "Don't cum yet, baby."

I sat there, stunned, trying to hold my shit back, as he said. When he lifted me from the counter, and lowered me on his dick, I almost ascended into Glory. The passion between us was off the charts already. While I was trying to gain stamina, this nigga was letting me know, off the top, that he could handle a big girl any way he wanted to. I was down with that shit, for real. After his second pump, I was on the edge. "Babyyyy, can I cum? Please?"

"Fuck! Yeah, girl. All over yo' shit."

And I let it loose. It was so overwhelming, I was no good for the position he had me in. My hips were refusing to cooperate. Regardless of how strong he was, if I couldn't cooperate, he'd get tired faster. So, I slid from his grasp, watching his dick bounce into his stomach. I went to my knees and sucked his balls, then licked up his shaft. His encouragement always made me go harder, even if he didn't say a word. When my lips touched the head, he grabbed my hair and pulled my head back. Zayson loved to see his dick leave my mouth. Then, he would ease it back in. True to form, when he did, I tried to swallow his shit. "Yeah, baby. Gag on yo' shit," he said roughly.

As my throat tightened around him, his body shuddered, then he said, "You want this shit?"

I moaned, "Mmm hmmm."

Within seconds, he released, giving me heaven in liquid form to digest into my soul. After draining him dry, he roughly lifted me from the floor and slid me back on the countertop, on my stomach. Pushing his monster back inside me, he had me trying to bear crawl away from it. Zayson grabbed my hips and held me to him. "Where you tryna go with my Sundae, girl? I only decorated the outside. Let him get in there and paint them walls."

"Zaaayyy... shit!"

He continued to pound into me until he couldn't hold back any longer. The growl that left him, as he released, made me flinch. I wasn't expecting that much passion to leave him that way. He leaned over and kissed my back, then helped me down. My legs were wobbly as hell, and I stumbled as I headed to the bathroom. Zayson chuckled, so I turned to him. "Something funny?"

"Yep. You look like a foal trying to stand for the first time." I frowned, so he clarified. "A baby horse."

"Hush, Zay. I feel like you worked me over like that poor colt you were training."

"Naw. That shit ain't mine. I'm way more delicate with my shit."

"Oh, yeah? Well, come in here and show me some tenderness, big daddy."

"Keep talking like that and tenderness gon' be the last thing you gon' get."

I giggled as he followed me to the bathroom. Nothing was going to break our bond if we didn't allow it to. The fact that he'd come back so quickly, to apologize and make up, let me know just how much he loved me... just how much he cared about making things right. J'Neka was lucky, because when I finally approached her again, I'd be a lot milder. She definitely wasn't completely off the hook, though.

Chapter Twenty

Z ayson

SINCE OUR LAST ARGUMENT, EVERYTHING HAD BEEN GOING well. Kortlynn and I had been working out, riding horses and hanging out, quite a bit, with Legend and Red and their wives. Not to mention, I'd been destroying them insides every chance I got. Baby girl had lost almost thirty pounds and it had only been two months since we'd been working out together. She was on her shit and I loved that. I could really tell the difference when we had sex. She was lasting longer and longer before getting tired. She even seemed like she felt better. After she told me that she was borderline diabetic, I stayed on her ass about eating right and working out.

The biggest goal was for her to be healthy. I could care less about her weight, if she was healthy, but the weight was causing her body to break down. We had to fix that. She was hating that she'd even told me about her health issues, because I'd become her personal trainer after that. Shiiid, more like a commander in bootcamp. The only thing I didn't do was curse at her. I would never belittle her, but I definitely pushed her... hard.

As I went outside, to work on a horse I was training for a bulldogger, my phone rang. Seeing it was my baby, I looked at the time. It was Thursday, which was the day I brought her lunch to the cancer treatment facility, but I'd also been staying the rest of the evening, with them, for support. Her dad had lost a lot of weight and I was worried about her emotional well-being. "Hello?"

"Hey, baby. Guess what?"

"What's up?"

"Serita just called me. Her ex-husband didn't donate the money, but he got his brother-in-law, Corey, to donate half a million dollars. He owns the Infiniti dealership on IH-10. Can you believe that?"

"Damn! Sheffield Infiniti?"

"Yes! I'm so excited, I had to come outside and call you!"

"I'm excited for you, baby. I know you didn't want to have to look for another job. Your passion is there."

"It really is. God is so good. Now, if He can spare my daddy, I'll be over the moon happy."

"I know, baby. But let me finish this session with this horse, so I can take a shower and come meet you."

"Okay. Love you!"

"Love you, too! We'll go out and celebrate tonight."

"Yay! Okay."

I ended the call. Hearing her so excited about her job working out put a smile on my face. While she was good at hiding it, I knew she cried at night, while praying for her daddy. Her eyes seemed to have a permanent puffiness about them now. But at least she didn't have to worry about her job. Serita had kept her there longer until she could hear from her ex-husband against her sisters' advice. She really valued Kortlynn and the work she was doing.

I'd started showing the girls how to garden and they seemed to be catching on. According to Kortlynn, they just wanted to watch me. I couldn't do a thing but shake my head and laugh. What could I say? Women of all ages loved me. Tomorrow, I would be back there to watch them water and check the crop. We'd planted tomatoes, bell peppers, cucumbers and cabbage. The first crop was good, but it could have been better. Some bugs had gotten to the tomatoes, so I explained to them how that wasn't a good thing and we had to get an insecticide that would be safe for our crop.

Once I was done riding the horse, trying to teach him the process of staying close to the steer, along with Red riding as the hazer, I went in the house and hurriedly took a shower. I was running behind schedule as usual. Rushing through it, I quickly got dressed and headed to Beaumont. I stopped to Fuzzy's Taco Shop and got some fish tacos, then went to the facility. Thursdays were tough enough on me so, after today, I decided as long as Kortlynn's dad was going through chemo and radiation, I wouldn't work out any animals. It was just too hard on me.

When I got there, Kortlynn was outside pacing. *Aww, shit.* Things had been going well too long. Only two people could get her thirty-eight hot like that. It was either her mama, or she'd come in contact with J'Neka. But I'd be willing to bet it had something to do with her mama. I parked and, the minute she saw me, she came to the truck and got in before I could get out. "I'm gon' kill those bitches."

"What?"

"I'm gon' kill those bitches, especially the older one."

"Who? What bitches?"

"Mary Hebert and J'Neka Hebert."

"Baby, calm down for a minute. Tell me what happened."

"Mary gold digging Hebert, left her phone here. She doesn't have a passcode. When I grabbed it to put in my purse to bring to her, she got a text from J'Neka, asking if she'd heard from me, and if we were still together. That shit only made me go looking for more text messages. My mother encouraged my cousin to come on to you."

My eyebrows lifted. I couldn't have heard her right. There was no way she said what I thought she said. "What? I know you didn't say what I think you said."

"Oh, you heard me correctly. Mary told J'Neka to flirt with you that day, at her house, when Aunt Rose was cooking. Remember when everyone had gon' to the kitchen and left us alone? That's when they started plotting."

"What the fuck? What kinda bullshit yo' mama on?"

"That's why that bitch still hadn't called your brother. She was too fucking busy trying to fuck you. I got something for both their asses, though. And I'm bringing Aunt Rose with me. Shit finna hit the fan and I need to know why my own fucking mama don't want me to be happy. I wanna know why it feels like she hates me."

"Baby, you can deal with that shit another time. I know you angry, but let's go back inside and focus on your dad. Okay? He needs us."

"You're right."

I kissed her lips and could feel the anger surging through her. She was about to get out the truck, but I grabbed her arm and pulled her back to me, kissing her until she let that shit go. There was a sudden exhale and I knew she'd dropped it, for now. Her hands flew to my head and she pulled me in deeper, as her tongue did a passionate dance with mine. When she let me go, her nose was red. I was almost sure mine was, too. "I'm gon' need you to fuck this outta me later."

"Gladly."

We got out of the truck and went inside the facility to find her dad sleeping. "Was he asleep when you left out?"

"Yeah."

Staring at him, I needed to see his chest still rising and falling. I believed today would be his last round of radiation and he had two or three more Thursdays of chemo. When I saw him inhale deeply and exhale, I relaxed and sat next to my baby. I held her hand in mine and silently prayed that she didn't lose him, especially not now. Besides her Aunt Rose and Legend, her dad was all she had that acted like he gave a damn about her. I'd never met J'Neka's parents and I was pretty sure I wouldn't.

She laid her head on my shoulder and I kissed her forehead, then whispered in her ear. "Don't tell your dad about this. He doesn't need the added stress."

Looking up at me, Kortlynn nodded her head. "No, he doesn't. He's dealing with enough already. Plus, he would only try to talk me out of having this conversation with mama. He hates confrontation and, normally, I'm the same way. It's probably why my mama has behaved the way she has, for years. I always shied away from it. But those days are over. I'm sick of this bullshit."

"I know, baby. It will get handled. Don't worry."

As I stroked her arm, she laid back on my shoulder. I thought my family was fucked up. The only problem was my brother, and no one took his side. While my parents wouldn't totally wash their hands of his ass, they still told him about himself. This situation, with her mama and her cousin, was some underhanded shit that required a certain level of jealousy, hatred and evilness to even accomplish half the shit her mama had done. I almost wanted to be there for the come to Jesus meeting. This whole situation was beyond my comprehension.

As we sat there in silence, a nurse approached us. "Hello, Ms. Kortlynn. I need to talk to you about something."

"It's okay, Ms. Nancy. This is my boyfriend, Zayson. Zayson, Ms. Nancy is usually leaving an hour after I get here."

I nodded my head, as the nurse nervously did the same. "I really don't know how to say this. Maybe the two of you should come over here."

I nodded at Kortlynn. It was probably something she didn't want Mr. Calvin to overhear. When we walked across the room, she looked at me, then Kortlynn, as we gave her our undivided attention. "Ms. Kortlynn, the blood you donated, for your dad's transfusion, isn't a match."

"What?"

"It is possible to have a different blood type. That doesn't disprove paternity, but you may want to do a DNA test."

"Can y'all do that here?"

"We normally don't, but I can... uh... do one for you," she said in a softer voice. "We can have the results back as soon as Monday, next week."

"That's bullshit. Just another reason for me to go off on her. If this man isn't my father, I'm gonna lose it on her ass."

"Baby, listen. Mr. Calvin will always be your father, regardless of the test results. I can't say that I know what any of this feels like, but I'm here for you. Okay?"

She nodded her head and told the nurse thank you. We walked back over to her dad who, thankfully, was still asleep. This was some crazy ass shit and I couldn't wait to get back to the simple ass living of the country.

⚜

INSTEAD OF GOING OUT TO CELEBRATE HER STILL HAVING A JOB, Kortlynn was just ready to get to my house. She stayed every Thursday night, because we usually worked out together. We worked out on Tuesday, Thursday and Saturdays. Sometimes, we worked out another day during the week as well. She said she needed to work off the aggression and there were no better ways than working out and fucking. She was getting a dirty mouth, hanging around my ass all the time. I liked that shit, though, especially when I was filling her with this prime beef. She cursed me out, all the time, during sex. That shit only made me go harder.

I was pretty sure sex was gon' be some wild type of shit tonight because of all the bullshit that had gone down. It was like her good news was overshadowed by so much negative shit, she'd forgotten all about it. As we lifted the machine weights, I asked, "So, you wanna go out, tomorrow night, to celebrate?"

"Celebrate what?"

"Baby... You'll still be at Integrity. Don't let all this bullshit take your joy. You already know that J'Neka is a triflin' ass bitch. You know that your mama don't want to see you happy. And, again, regardless of how that test comes out, Calvin is your father. Let's put all that negativity out of your mind, for now. I know it will have to be addressed, eventually, but today ain't the day for it. Let's put in this work, take a shower and put in some more work. Then, we can eat a lil something and carry our asses to bed. You feel me?"

"Yep. Let's get it."

She started lifting again, but I could still see the anger inside of her. That was okay, though. She was gon' sleep like a baby when I got through with her.

Chapter Twenty-One

K ortlynn

ZAYSON COULD CALM ME DOWN, NO MATTER THE SITUATION.
However, this situation with my mama and J'Neka was fueling my
anger and I felt like I would hurt the both of them. That's why I knew
Aunt Rose had to come with me. My mama hadn't tried to contact
me, by any other means, about her phone and I think it was because
she knew I'd probably seen the text messages between her and
J'Neka. I couldn't wait to get to the bottom of this shit, so I could go
back to my peaceful life.

Zay and I had gone out Friday night and had an amazing time at
Suga's. Then, Saturday, he'd taken me to a local rodeo, so I could see
the event he and Red would be participating in. It was really interest-
ing. And, for the first time, I got to see Legend ride. I, now, knew why
they called him the living Legend. He was unbelievably good. Red
was just as amazing. They both won their events and I also spent a

little time with Harper, selling her baked goodies. Her banana pudding cupcakes were delicious. When she'd brought them to my mama's house, for that unforgettably disastrous dinner, I'd fallen in love with them.

Sunday, per usual, I'd gone to church with Zay and his family, then went to dinner at his parents' house. My weekend had been so busy, I hadn't had time to think about my troubles. Zayson had put that shit down on me so good, this weekend, I couldn't really think about shit else, as long as I was around him. His mama had cracked jokes, while we were in the kitchen alone, saying how I'd let Zay get a taste. I was so damn embarrassed. She eventually made me feel comfortable to where I even admitted it and told her she was late to the party. She really had a field day with me after that. Mrs. Barbara was quickly becoming my confidant and I enjoyed spending time with her.

As I sat at my desk, all I could think about were those fucking test results. Ms. Nancy said they would have the results today. I needed the proof, but already knew that he probably wasn't my father. I didn't look a thing like him, and I didn't look like Mary either. She claimed I looked like my deceased grandmother but, according to the pictures I'd seen of her, I didn't look like her either, in my opinion. I just didn't feel that in my heart, either. I had always suspected that there was someone else that had probably hit it and quit it and she blamed it on my dad because he had more money.

The anxiety was killing me, so I decided to call Mrs. Barbara to help me calm my nerves. Her phone rang three times, so I was about to end the call, when she answered. "Hello?"

"Hey, Mrs. Barbara. How are you today?"

"Kortlynn! Hey, D-I-L!"

She called me D-I-L, which was short for daughter-in-law. I found myself smiling, every time she did. Of course, she didn't fail to point that out to me yesterday at Sunday dinner. "Hey. I need to talk to you about something that's been heavy on me all weekend."

"Oh, shit. Zay didn't mess up, did he?"

I giggled a little. "Zay has been perfect. This is about something else."

"Whew! He can't be messing up my plans." She laughed, but I didn't join her. After abruptly stopping, she asked, "What's on your mind, sweetness?"

"Thursday, the nurse told me that the blood I donated for my daddy's transfusion wasn't a match. In my heart, I know he's not my biological daddy. I can feel it in my soul. I haven't gotten the results of the DNA test yet, but I should have them some time today. The problem will be trying to contain myself when I confront my mother."

"You feel betrayed, lied to and misled. I get that. But if you've always felt that way, don't let the proof take you out of character. Hear your mother out. She may have a legitimate reason for what she did or why she told you that he was your father. I know it seems like no excuse will be good enough, but don't fly off the handle before you give her a chance to explain."

"So, if I'm not feeling her explanation, then I go off."

"Go the hell off! Just don't go too far, baby. That has to be a painful thing. It makes you feel like you don't know who you are."

Damn, she understood everything I was feeling, without me even saying the shit. I was glad I called her, because I was already feeling better about things. All those years my dad agreed to pay child support, made me wonder if he knew. Why would you pay child support for a kid without a paternity test? Especially if you and the mother weren't in a relationship. Everything I'd grown up believing all felt like a lie. I must had been quiet for a while, because she asked, "You okay, sweetie?"

"Yes, ma'am. I was just thinking about how you summed up exactly how I felt about this issue. For all I know, Zayson could be related to me."

"Oh, hell no! Don't even say no shit like that!"

I laughed loudly and she joined in. That would be some bullshit.

We talked a little longer and I finally ended the call to go check on the girls. Zayson had to practice with Red, since he'd taken the whole weekend off for me, so I'd refrained from calling so much. I'd also told him I would make sure the girls were doing what they were supposed to, which was mainly watering the vegetables they'd planted. The girls had been pretty rowdy, at this summer camp. Some of them had me questioning why I wanted to stay here. I knew they were the ones who needed our influence the most, but this one lil girl was gon' make me lose my job.

When I got outside, one of the instructors was out there with them, as they watered the crop. The main thorn in my flesh saw me and immediately asked, "Where's Zayson, with his fine ass?"

Before I could even address her, the instructor jumped all over her, then sent her inside. "This is your last warning, before you get kicked out of the program!"

The girl rolled her eyes and proceeded inside, as the instructor looked at me. "You okay?"

"Yeah. I was two seconds from being on her like white in a snowstorm."

"I felt that. I could see it in your face. If you didn't need your job, she would have gotten everything you had for her."

I chuckled, as did she. "Thanks."

I took a few pictures with my phone and sent them to Zay, then went back inside. This heat was going to kill me this summer. Walking back inside, I was already sweating. I sat at my desk and resumed some paperwork but noticed a small bouquet of flowers on a side table. I smiled, then walked to them. They were some beautiful sunflowers in a glass vase. Grabbing the card from the stem, I nearly stopped breathing when I read it.

We got off to a wrong start, and I know that was my fault. I apologize for being a jackass. I can see how much my brother loves you and how important you are to him. Can we start over?
Kerry

Shut the fuck up. I took a picture of the card and sent it to Zay. Within seconds, he was calling. I giggled, then answered. "Hey."

"What the fuck he up to? I'm gon' have to call my mama about this. What kind of flowers did he buy? Better not be no roses."

The name of the florist was on the card. "No. Sunflowers."

Zayson was quiet as hell, before finally saying, "Let me call you back."

He ended the call and I went back to my paperwork, wondering why it was such a big deal. I thought it was a nice gesture to repair what he'd damaged. And, he'd actually apologized, something Zay said he never did. I didn't question it, though, because he knew his brother. My phone began ringing again, and I knew if I kept answering it, there was no way I would get out of here at five. "Hello?"

"Hi. Ms. Kortlynn?"

"Yes?"

"This is Nancy at the cancer treatment facility. I have your results."

My heart was beating erratically, as I sat straight up in my chair, like I was trying to maintain good posture. She continued, "Did you want to come get the results today?"

"I will get them some time this week. Probably Thursday. If at all possible, could you tell me?"

"I'm so sorry, Kortlynn, but he's not your father."

My eyes closed, as she confirmed what I already knew. Swallowing the lump in my throat, I exhaled slowly. "Okay. Thank you, Ms. Nancy. I appreciate you doing that for me."

"No problem. If you need anything, let me know."

"Yes, ma'am. Thank you."

I ended the call, then sat motionless at my desk. How could my mama do this? She probably never thought I would find out, but this was a horrible way to find out the truth. It would have been a lot easier for her to sit me down and talk to me, even if she would have waited until I was an adult to do so. Having to find out for myself stung. It was like the breath had been sucked out of me.

After being at work all day, and not leaving until after six, I was exhausted. I'd talked to Zayson again about his brother. He'd said that he seemed genuine, but he would be keeping his eye on him. I'd chuckled about it, then I told him about my DNA results. I was so down, I didn't feel like doing much of anything when I got home. I fixed myself a sandwich, then took a shower. I suppose some part of me was hoping that he *was* my biological father, even when logic said he wasn't. Before I could crawl in the bed, there was a knock at my door.

Walking down the hallway, I did my best to pull some positive vibes from within me, because sadness was taking over me. The anger had turned into hurt and I was having a hard time dealing with it. I knew I needed to talk to my mama, sooner rather than later, and I needed to call Aunt Rose, but my heart was so broken, I just wanted to be, for now. Looking through the peephole, I saw my baby, standing there with a box and some flowers.

After opening the door, he came in and sat everything on the table and immediately pulled me in his arms. "I'm sorry, baby."

Zayson kissed my forehead, then my lips, sending chills all over my body and led me to the table. "I know you're dieting, but I felt like you could stand a cheat day. I brought you some mini cupcakes from Gigi's and... Oh, shit. I left it in the truck. I'll be right back."

I smiled at him, as he ran out the door. Zayson always knew how to pull me out of my despair. I sat at the bar and opened the box of cupcakes. They smelled divine but I knew I had to take this slow. My body wanted all four of them, but I knew I had better only eat one. When Zayson came back inside, he was holding a Sonic cup. "I know you like the Fanta Orange with strawberry and lemonade, so I got you that. Now, don't relapse on me. This is just comfort food."

"You're all the comfort I need, baby."

He sat next to me, and gently stroked my back, then grabbed a lemon-flavored cupcake and fed it to me slowly, between kisses to my lips. After the last bite, Zayson pulled me closer and licked the icing from my lips. "Come on, baby."

He helped me to my feet, then put my drink in the fridge. We went to my bedroom and he held me in his arms until I was fast asleep.

Chapter Twenty-Two

Z ayson

Baby girl was so down yesterday, but I knew that would wear off. I did my best to comfort her and offer her peace. Her mind had to be going crazy with how she would approach her mama about lying to her. Not only that, but her trying to tear me and Kortlynn apart was baffling to me. My mama told me that Kort had called her to ask for advice on the situation and how she should approach her mother. I liked that they were getting so close.

Kortlynn had been super emotional with me but tears never came. I knew she was trying to be strong, but I could see the pain in her eyes. Her pain was heavy, and I could feel it every time I held her in my arms. My job was to alleviate as much of her pain as I could. I'd called my brother, then went to his house to confront him about the flowers. I didn't know what had happened, but that nigga was sensitive as hell. He was apologizing for all kinds of shit. I was willing to bet he'd gotten the shaft on that racehorse. I'd find out sooner or later what this shit was about.

After practicing with Red, for a couple of hours, I took a shower and went to the center. When I got there, the girls were walking outside. I could hear them yelling, as I walked around the building. "Zayson's here!"

Kortlynn rolled her eyes as they ran to me to shake my hand. They used to try to hug me, but I shut that shit down quick. The last lil girl shook my hand slow. "Hi, Zayson."

I pulled my hand from hers. "What's up?"

"You."

I frowned as I made my way to the group. They were looking at the green tomatoes and picking with them. "Don't pick with it y'all. You gon' make them break off the stem."

They stepped back and I noticed that lil girl staring at me. She was making me uncomfortable as hell. Kortlynn had seen our exchange and the frown that made its way to her face made me uncomfortable as well. She looked like she wanted to fuck that girl up. I had to keep reminding myself that she was a kid, because she looked twenty-five or older, but she was only sixteen. Once we'd looked at the crop and watered it, we went back inside.

Serita was standing there to help corral the girls. It was a good thing, too, because I knew Kortlynn was gon' tell that girl something. "Aye, baby. I gotta go. I have to go ride that mare."

"Okay. Aunt Rose is meeting me at my mama's house, when I get off."

"Oh, shit. Try not to do or say anything that you will regret once you cool off. Okay?"

"Yeah. That's why I have Aunt Rose coming with me, to kind of keep me in line. Mom knows that I know, because she still has yet to call me about her phone. She had to have reported it lost and got another one, because this shit ain't rang since the day after I found it."

"Mrs. Semien can get rowdy, too. I don't know how she gon' keep you in line when she probably gon' hop over that shit herself."

156

She giggled as my phone rang. I ignored it. I'd call whomever it was when I left. "Well, go ahead, baby. I have a lot of paperwork to do. We're working to get our funding back. It's imperative that we get more money coming in because, eventually, that donation is gonna run out."

"Okay, baby. Call me before you go and as soon as you leave."

"Okay. I love you, Zay."

"I love you, too, baby."

I kissed her lips, then left her standing in the doorway to her office. Before I could get out the door, I heard, "Byyyyye, Zaysoooon."

I turned in the direction the voice came from and saw that girl, along with Kortlynn heading toward her. Walking to the girl, I could see the excitement on her face. She just didn't know. I was about to save her life and Kortlynn's job all at the same time. Stepping in front of her, in the nick of time, Kortlynn said, "Go to Ms. Taylor's office. Today will be your last day in the program."

She rolled her eyes at Kortlynn. "I doubt it, but I'll go to her office."

When she walked away, I moved in front of Kortlynn. "That's a lil girl. You can't fuck her up and get fired."

"Yeah, yeah. I know. Get out of here, so you can get some work done."

I shook my head at her, as I twisted my lips sideways, then walked out the door. Once inside my truck, I looked at my phone to see I'd missed a call from Kerry. *What in the hell did he want?* I guess I was gon' find out, on my way home, because I was too nosy to let the shit be. Dialing the number back, he answered on the first ring. "Man, I fucked up."

"What's going on?"

"I fucked him up bad. He ain't moving. I think I killed him. Shit! Shit!"

I'd never heard Kerry in such a state of panic like this. I suppose I would be panicking, too, if I thought I killed somebody. "What? Who? What the fuck, Kerry?"

"The muthafucka I did business with was trying to screw me out of the seventy grand I put up for the horse. He said that the horse injured his leg and was done. I decided to go by there, unannounced, and saw the horse running just fine. When I approached him, the nigga had the nerve to run. I chased his ass down and beat the shit out of him."

"Damn, Kerry! Did you call 9-1-1?"

"No. I'm scared as shit. I don't wanna got to jail, man. I should've listened to y'all... to Mama and Daddy."

"Call 9-1-1. Where are you?"

"I'm at his place, in Westbury."

He gave me the address so I could put it in my navigation. I couldn't believe this nigga was in all this trouble. Although he didn't want me to, I called Mama and Daddy anyway. Mama was hysterical and Daddy was having a hard time calming her down. I didn't need him to have a heart attack either. "Mama, please calm down. Think about Daddy and his medical condition. Kerry got himself in the position he's in. All we can do is pray that this guy isn't dead."

"Zayson! Don't put yourself in harm's way to see about his ass. If the police aren't there yet, don't go in there. Kerry could be trying to set you up. You hear me?"

"Yes, ma'am."

"Call us when you get there," my dad added.

"Yes, sir."

All this fucking drama. I hated it. Although none of it had to do with me and Kortlynn, it was still wearing on my nerves. It was why I didn't do drama with Kortlynn and she was the same way. She was on her positive energy shit and tried to stay away from negativity, but the shit was unavoidable. When I got to the house, I didn't see Kerry's truck. I slow rolled by the place and called his phone. He didn't answer. Mama was probably right. He wouldn't have to worry about going to jail, because I was gon' kill his ass. That muthafucka sent those flowers to Kortlynn so I would let my guard down about him.

He'd probably never called the police, but I was about to call.

There was no way I could let a man possibly die by himself. It was possible that he could still be alive and needed some help. However, I knew if got out of my vehicle, they were gonna arrest me automatically. "9-1-1, can I help you?"

"My brother called me, hysterical, thinking he'd possibly killed a man in Westbury. He gave me the address he was at and I told him to call 9-1-1. However, when I got here, the police weren't here and neither was he. I'm assuming he never called, so I'm calling now."

"Is the man breathing?"

"I don't know. I'm not next to him. I didn't want to go on the premises until the police got here."

"Okay. A car is on its way, along with an ambulance."

"Thank you."

I ended the call, then tried to call my punk ass brother again. That nigga still didn't answer the phone. When I called my mama back to tell her that that nigga wasn't here, she really lost it. Not that she didn't love me and Kerry the same, but I was her baby. I'd always been the responsible one, even though Kerry was three years older than me. I spent more time with them and did more for them, so she naturally gravitated to me more. She didn't want to see me get in trouble, especially for something Kerry did. Not long after I ended the call, the police cars were flying up. Two of the officers went on the premises, with their guns drawn, and another approached my truck with his weapon drawn as well. I knew not to make any sudden movements and put my hands on the steering wheel. When he got close to the truck, he yelled, "Put your window down and your hands on the steering wheel."

I did as I was told, and he approached the window. "Aww, shit. Zayson, what are you doing here?"

The cop was someone I'd gone to school with. He put his gun back in the holster, as I told him about the phone call from Kerry. He shook his head, almost the entire time, as the ambulance drove up. "Dispatch told us someone else had called in but had hung up before the call could be traced. Okay. They'll probably need you to answer some questions."

"Okay."

When the ambulance went in, with a gurney, and came back out with the man stretched out on it, I breathed out a sigh of relief. He wasn't dead, but Kerry could definitely get charged with assault. He'd fucked this dude up. I was willing to bet he had broken bones. The other officers approached me and they began questioning me. I hesitated when I gave them my brother's address and I felt like a fucking snitch, but it was either him or me and it sure in the hell wouldn't be me.

Once I'd answered all their questions, they sped off to try to find Kerry. I still couldn't believe he'd done me like that. He was depending on me to get out the truck and get caught with that man. I'd never thought he would stoop so low to set me up like that. Hate like that ran deep. The crazy part about it was that I'd never done anything to him but love him as my big brother. When I was in the ninth grade, I remember telling everybody that Kerry Ardoin, the popular basketball player was my brother. I looked up to him and admired everything about him. So much so, I tried to emulate everything he did.

Our troubles started when his girlfriend, who was in the eleventh grade, tried to fuck me. I didn't want that ol' trout mouth goat, but he'd thought that I was trying to holla at her on the cool. And that was why she wanted to fuck me. It was nothing for me to walk out the locker room with just some shorts on that showed my dick print. The girls would stare at the sight before them, giggle and lick their lips, his girlfriend included. One day, he caught her looking at me, in an unacceptable fashion, and blamed me, like I could control her eyes. We'd been distant ever since.

When I got home, I went straight to that mare, which was a female horse. I had work to do and, because of Kerry's trifling ass, I was three fucking hours behind. Kortlynn would be calling in an hour or so, when she got off. Pushing Kerry out of my mind, I thought about how hard this would be for Kortlynn. Not only did she have to approach her mom about the DNA results, but she also had to deal with her and J'Neka's fucked-up plan to keep her as an old maid.

I could feel her heart was heavy. Instead of doing what I intended to do, I got off the horse and went in the house to take a shower. When she got back home, I would be there waiting for her. She was gonna need me to hold her after this shit. I prayed for her strength, self-control and peace. Mrs. Semien could only stop so much before she tired out. Kortlynn was getting strong as hell these days. I took deep breaths, trying to calm my ass down about the situation. While I wanted to be there with her, I knew it was something she needed to do on her own. I'd just be there to pick up the pieces with her favorite flowers, dinner and a bottle of wine. Then, she'd get to see the stars when she boarded the rocket.

Chapter Twenty-Three

K ortlynn

"Thank you, Aunt Rose, for meeting me here," I said as I hugged her.

My entire body was trembling, and Aunt Rose did nothing to relieve it. After I told her everything I knew, she was ready to wring my mama's neck. Aunt Rose said that she'd called J'Neka and told her to be here as well. It was gonna take an army to stop me from beating her ass. She'd better hope that my positive energy took over, 'cause, right now, I wanted to slap the shit out of both of them. Then, I thought about what Mrs. Barbara had said to me.

Taking deep breaths, I knocked on her door, as Aunt Rose grabbed my other hand. Either she was nervous or just as mad as I was because her hand was trembling. Soon after, my mama opened the door and immediately looked at our joined hands. She didn't bother to speak, just stepped aside to let us inside. When I saw

J'Neka, I wanted to charge at her ass like I was Bobby Boucher on the football field.

Instead, I sat on the love seat, while she fidgeted on the sofa. Aunt Rose sat beside me, and when my mama sat next J'Neka, I fished my mother's phone out of my purse. "Kortlynn! You had my phone this whole time? I reported it lost and got another one."

I didn't give her the satisfaction of a response, just held it out to her. She knew I had it. That was why she hadn't called me since last week. That was also why she was walking on eggshells, because she didn't know what I knew. After grabbing it from me, she asked, "So, what do we need to talk about?"

I didn't waste any time getting down to it. "First on the agenda is the messages between you and J'Neka, on that phone."

I glanced at J'Neka and her face was red as hell. "What messages are you talking about Kortlynn?"

"Don't patronize me, Mom. You know exactly what messages I'm talking about. Why did you have her come on to Zayson?"

She took a deep breath and the fact that she was taking so long to answer the question was making me angrier. She finally spit out, "I did that to protect you. I wanted to see if he would fall to temptation. You aren't the perfect shape, and I didn't want him leading you on to think you were it for him when he had ill intentions."

"First of all, Zayson loves me just the way I am. He's genuine. Secondly, I don't need you looking out for me. I'm thirty-two years old and very capable of sniffing out bullshit. Thirdly, I think you need counseling, the both of you, if you are that jealous of my relationship with Zay that you feel like you have to try to destroy it. This has nothing to do with you trying to protect me, but everything to do with how you can't believe the big girl has found a love so sweet before the two of you."

"He's going to mess up and I can't wait to tell you I told you so."

"Well, you may as well swallow and digest that shit, because we're better than good." I turned my attention to J'Neka. "And I been should have stopped hanging with your hoe ass. Even if my mama asked you to do that, you have a mind of your own. You could have said no. But, that lets me know you wanted to do that shit. I watched you manipulate and play people, over the years, but I never would have thought you would have done that shit to me."

"I'm sorry, Kortlynn. I let money and lust cloud my judgement. I'm not going to say that I didn't give Zay a once-over, or that I didn't think he was extremely attractive but, trying to sleep with him hadn't crossed my mind. I only have a little longer to get my doctorate and any amount of money could help with that. Daddy is struggling, trying to pay for everything. So, when I was offered two grand to see how loyal Zayson was to you, I jumped all over the opportunity."

I reached across the table and slapped the piss out of her. She didn't move one inch to defend herself. Her scholarship was only for four years and it had taken her a little longer to finish. She wouldn't have any scholarship money for next semester. Briefly, I felt sorry for her, but that wasn't a logical excuse. Since I didn't attempt to slap her again, no one moved. "J'Neka, that is the lamest excuse I've ever heard. You could have gotten a summer job and saved money. You have a master's degree. I'm more than sure you could have worked somewhere. Some part of you is jealous of what I have. I don't care how desperate you are for money, you wouldn't turn your back on family, unless you wanted to."

Dropping her head, she began fidgeting again while my mother sat there like a church mouse. Aunt Rose squeezed my hand, as I struggled getting out the next part. "I also had a DNA test done on me and my daddy."

Her head snapped up. "Why would you do that?"

"I donated blood for his transfusion. It turns out that I wasn't a match. I found that to be unusual, so I had them run a DNA test on our samples. The results came back Monday. He's not my father. In my mind, I feel like you knew he wasn't the father. But, all these years, you lied to me, like I didn't deserve the truth. That shit hurt! Do you even know who my father is?"

"Calvin is your dad. Whether he's biological or not, that's your daddy."

"Mom, don't try me. That man has been in my life almost twenty years. Helping take care of a kid that didn't belong to him. He was paying child support."

"You don't know what you're talking about, Kortlynn, so just shut up."

"Hell, no. You gon' spit that shit out, Mary. You so shut off from everybody. I feel like whatever the problem is, as to why you're so reserved, is the same problem that kept you from telling Kortlynn about her father. Talking out our problems heals us. You can't keep all of that bottled in."

Mama sat there fidgeting again. "Calvin knows he's not your biological dad."

"What?"

"When I told him I was pregnant, we hadn't had sex in months. He said he would help me, and he put himself on child support. He didn't want to be involved, like that, with raising a child, though. He had a lot going on at the time. So, by the time you were ten, he asked if he could be in your life as your father. I told him yes, but I would have to pretend to be scorned if I was gonna introduce him to you as your father."

I was silent for a moment. Why in the hell would he do that? That was something he didn't have to do. "Why would he do that? Who's my biological dad?"

She was silent for a while, then she lowered her head to her hands and cried. Aunt Rose and I looked at one another. I'd rarely seen my mama emotional. She'd always presented this strong front like she was unfuckwithable and nothing bothered her. I didn't move for a while because I didn't know how to take it. Consoling her was something I'd never had to do. Aunt Rose stood from her seat and sat next to my mama. "So, the story about trapping Calvin by poking pinholes in the condom wasn't true, was it?"

Mama shook her head. God, what was it? What was tearing her

apart like this? J'Neka was sitting there crying, as well, like she knew something. I did my best to ignore her, though, because I still wanted to pop her in her mouth. Giving my attention back to my mom, who was finally pulling herself together, I fidgeted in my seat, trying to prepare myself for whatever she had to say. She looked up at me, with tears in her eyes. "Kortlynn, you are the product of a rape."

My eyebrows lifted and my heart dropped to my feet. Although I was trying to prepare myself for what she had to say, that shit knocked the wind out of me. I was stunned and trying to find the words to say in response to what she'd said. All I could stammer out was, "What?"

"I was raped. Rose, your ex-boyfriend raped me. I was only seventeen when it happened. I'd seen him, in the store, and he asked to take me out. I told him no, because he was your ex. I would have never betrayed you that way. He had other plans, though. As I was walking down the alley, to get home, he snatched me in the bushes and told me I was gonna give him everything you didn't. He tore off my linen shorts and had his way with me. I wasn't a virgin, so it wasn't hard to hide. My body betrayed me, so the act wasn't as rough as it could have been. There was no bleeding or tearing."

She broke down again and, at that moment, the tears began falling from my eyes. I felt sorry for her and what she went through. Laying my hand on my chest, I listened to her as she continued. "When I got home, Mama saw my shorts were torn and that my hair was disheveled. I didn't say a word. She grabbed my hand and brought me to the bathroom and ran me a hot bath. I didn't understand what she was doing until she finally said that this sort of thing happened all the time and that I had to be strong and deal with it. When I found out I was pregnant, she wouldn't let me abort the pregnancy because she said that was wrong. So, I had to have you."

That was why she hated me. She was forced to look at her rapist, every day, when she looked at me. I clearly had to look like him, since I didn't look like her. God, my heart was heavy and all I could think about was running to Zayson. Aunt Rose was holding my mama while rocking and crying. Mama sat up and looked at me. What I saw in her eyes scared me for a moment. She said, "So, about two weeks after I graduated from high school, I had you. My mama held you in her arms and said we couldn't give up this beautiful baby. She said surely I could raise you to be an intelligent, self-sufficient young woman. That shit changed me forever. I'm sorry, Kortlynn, but I hated looking at you. Yes, you're beautiful, but you look just like him. I'd get sick to my stomach every time I looked in your big, beautiful eyes. It was so hard, but I got past it. I raised you to the best of my ability. I'm sorry, but I feel like I've never loved you."

I stood from my seat. It felt like she stabbed me in my heart with a damned machete. "Kortlynn, I'm sorry. I couldn't appreciate men after that. They thought they could just take whatever they wanted and wouldn't suffer consequences for it. Calvin was my first and I fell in love with him, but he didn't feel the same way about me. That's why he stopped messing around with me. Then, five months later, I got raped. That's why I always interfered with your relationships because men are no good! None of them! I wanted you to see that, too. You seem to be stuck on Zayson, though, so I had to do more."

I couldn't take anymore. I grabbed my purse, as Aunt Rose and my mama begged me not to leave. Getting out of there was imperative for me. I couldn't go there, in the depths of my emotions, with a woman that never loved me; that wanted me to be as miserable as she was. As I walked to the door, my mama ran to me. "Kortlynn, please forgive me! I wanted you to have love that I felt I couldn't give, that's why I let Calvin come into your life. God, I'm sorry!"

She'd fallen to her knees and held me around my legs. Her actions didn't say that she hated me. They actually said the opposite of everything she was telling me. She, at least, was exhibiting that she cared. But, because of the way she raised me to be, I needed to be with the only person that I knew loved me unconditionally. If I couldn't be with him, I'd rather be alone than sit here with her and J'Neka. "I forgive you, Mom. I just need to be alone."

She stood to her feet and hugged me tightly. Looking in her eyes, as they leaked her emotions onto her cheeks, I said, "Thank you for doing the best you could with me. You could have physically abused or neglected me."

I kissed her forehead, then left. It felt like I was suffocating. To know that she was raped, and I was the product of it, was heavy. I didn't know how she did it all those years. My grandmother should have been ashamed of herself. She didn't help her daughter heal from what had happened to her. She only threw salt in the wound. While I hated what she did to my mama, I was grateful she did, at the same time. Had she done what was right by her daughter, there was a chance that I might not be here.

When I got home, I was so emotionally exhausted. I drug myself up the stairs and, when I got to my door, I nearly collapsed. There stood my baby, leaning against the wall with a bouquet of flowers and a bottle of wine in his hand. He brought my favorite, Stella Rosa Black. That was gonna be empty before the night was over. Zayson put everything in one hand, then pulled me to him with his free hand. "You okay?"

I only shook my head in response, then unlocked the door, so we could go in. Once inside, I realized he had a bag hanging from his arm and I immediately smelled the Chinese food. My stomach started growling loudly. Zayson smirked at me and said, "Sounds like you hungry, girl. Come sit yo' fine ass down so I can feed you."

My face heated up, as I made my way to him at the bar. He helped me on the stool, then went to pour us glasses of wine. "So, I take it everything didn't go well."

"I'm the product of a rape. Daddy knows I'm not his daughter. He just wanted to help my mama, so he put himself on child support. Then, when he asked to be in my life, she let him."

"Damn, baby girl. That gotta be hard."

"What was harder was listening to my mama say that she feels like she's never loved me."

I swallowed the tears back as Zayson sat my glass of wine in front of me. He was staring at me, probably waiting for me to break down.

Instead, I picked up the glass and gulped it. He quickly poured me another one and I gulped it, too. After pouring another glass, Zay sat next to me and pulled me in his arms for a minute. "She allowed Calvin to come into my life to give me love that she couldn't give me. That was why she was so hard on me. I look like her rapist; the man that altered her life forever. How do I recover from that? I have a master's degree in family counseling, but this is overwhelming."

"I don't know, baby, but maybe Serita can help you. Just because you have a degree doesn't mean you should be able to help yourself. While they may diagnose their own problems, doctors don't perform their own surgeries. The only thing I know to do is to love you and be here for you, but maybe she can help by talking you through it. She is a licensed counselor, too, right?"

"Yeah."

He opened the combination rice and dipped the spoon in it. After saying grace, he brought it to my mouth. I thought my appetite had left but, as soon as I tasted my favorite indulgence, it quickly came back, like *here I am bitch.* My eyes closed and I leaned against his shoulder. He kissed my forehead, then ate some as well. He continued on, between the two of us, until we'd killed the entire platter and two eggrolls.

I stood from the stool and was heading to my bedroom until he stopped me. "Babe, chill out on the sofa. Let me get this shit prepared for you."

I gave him a slight smile, then sat on the couch, as he suggested. Zayson was so country but he was hood at the same damn time. The way he talked, you would think he grew up in the projects some-where. I loved that shit, though. As I sat there, thinking about him and how grateful I was to have him, he came back without a shirt on and helped me up from the sofa by grabbing my hand. After kissing his lips, I followed him to the bathroom and the sight almost took my breath away.

There were flower petals everywhere, candles were lit and he'd run me a bubble bath. I could hear Lalah Hathaway playing softly.

Turning back to him, I saw him taking off his pants and underwear. Thankfully, I had a nice sized air tub. This was amazing, though. Zayson pulled me close to him and began undressing me. All I could do was stare at him in awe. We'd never taken a bath together.

Once he was done, he led me to the tub. After he got in, he helped me in. Watching him ease down in the hot water was funny as hell, but I didn't laugh. He was trying to be romantic, so I didn't want to ruin the moment. When he'd finally sat, I eased down in the water, between his legs, and laid back against him. Wrapping his arms around my stomach, I exhaled slowly. Damn. I could lay here in this hot water, against him, all night. "Thank you, Zayson. I love you, baby."

"I love you, too, and I'm gonna do my best to love you through this. I know tomorrow will be hard as well, so I'll be with you all day. I brought clothes to spend the night."

Just his words had me crying uncontrollably. My body was shaking, as my emotions overtook me. I'd been trying to hold it in, but his genuine love and care for me took me over. "It's okay, baby. Let it out."

He gently rubbed my head and kissed it repeatedly. The way he loved me was almost unbelievable. My mama, who raised me, saw me every day, and that played a critical role in how I turned out, said she never loved me. But, this man, who hadn't even known me five months, loved me enough to take care of my heart. How?

Zayson washed my body slowly and sensuously, taking his time to massage me with his fingertips and kiss me in various spots. My eyes stayed closed, almost the whole time. Despite his rough demeanor, he was so tender with me, at times. When he finished, he began drying me off. "In other news, Kerry tried to set me up to catch a case."

My eyes widened. "What?"

"He beat some dude's ass about trying to con him out of that stupid ass racehorse he bought. He went to his house and found out he was lying. Well, after he beat his ass, he called me sounding all scared and shit, saying he thought the guy was dead. I told him to give me the address and I would come see about him. I also told him to call the police. When I got there, his ass had done left the scene, so it would look like I was guilty of something. Punk ass. I gave the police his address and, lucky for me, I knew a couple of the officers."

Damn. He was here taking care of me and he had all that shit on him, too. I turned to him and hugged him around his waist. "Let's just leave town and not tell anybody."

He chuckled. "If it wasn't for my parents, and your dad, I would probably take you up on that."

"I'm sorry, baby. That was lowdown, cold and heartless. Your own brother."

"Yep. But what can I do about it? Not a damn thing. I'll just move on. When he really needs me, I won't be there. If I have my way, I'll have a family to think about by then anyway."

My eyebrows went up slightly. "Really?"

"Yeah. It's this chick that I know. She so damn fine and confident and sexy. This girl got me feeling all kinds of shit that I ain't ever felt before. From the day I met her, I knew I didn't want to be without her. You might know her. She about yo' age, yo' height, yo' build and she works for Integrity."

"Yeah? What's her name?"

"One day, it'll be Mrs. Zayson James Ardoin. But, for now, it's Kortlynn Denise Hebert."

Damn. Zayson had turned me on, in ways unimaginable, by talking about our future. "Yeah, I know her. Sis fly as hell."

Zayson laughed loudly, then pulled me back to him. Being around one another made us better and I was certain that we could live in our own little bubble and be just fine.

Chapter Twenty-Four

Z ayson

It was awkward as hell walking in the cancer treatment center. Mr. Calvin didn't have a clue that Kortlynn knew what he and Ms. Mary had kept a secret for over twenty years. He was gonna find out today, though. I just prayed he didn't take it too hard. While all of the nurses and doctors were talking about how well he was doing, he looked just the opposite to us. He was small and frail-looking. When he saw us approaching, his face brightened. "Zayson! What are you doing here this early?"

I shook his hand and smiled back at him. "I took off to be with my baby, today."

He nodded and smiled. "Hey, baby girl. How are you?"

"I'm okay, Daddy. How are you feeling?"

"I feel okay, today, baby. It looks like something is bothering you, though. You sure you okay?"

Kortlynn glanced over at me, then sat next to her daddy. "Daddy, they'd asked me to donate some blood, because you needed a blood transfusion. Our blood type didn't match, so I had a DNA test done. I know, Daddy. I know everything."

I watched him lower his head. "I'm sorry you had to find out that way, baby. Well, I guess you know why I wasn't there the first ten years of your life and why your mama behaves the way she does."

"She told me, today, that she feels like she never loved me."

His eyes widened and he grabbed Kortlynn's hand. "Baby, your mom has some serious issues with what happened to her. I know she loves you. While she may have not been the best mom, she did her best to love and care for you to the best of her ability. She allowed me to come in to make up for what she may have been lacking. Don't let her sell you that wolf ticket."

Kortlynn only nodded her head in response to what he said. "What made you want to help her when you didn't even want to be with her?"

"She'd fallen in love with me, but I wasn't ready to settle down. I felt bad about hurting her feelings and I did care about her. I'd always told her, whenever she needed me, I would be there for her. So, when she called and told me what happened, and that she'd had a baby as a result, I felt bad for her. After ten years had passed, I decided that I wanted to be a dad to you. Mary was grateful to me for that and she told me why. She said she didn't feel like she was enough. So, try to understand where she's coming from."

I stood next to Kortlynn and stroked her back, as she took in everything her dad was saying. When they were done talking about the situation, and had hugged, I sat on the other side of him. I was glad their talk went well. What he did was honorable. Taking financial responsibility for a kid that wasn't his, then, going a step further and establishing a relationship with her was rare. Some men didn't want to take responsibility for kids that were theirs. They continued to hold hands while I kind of slumped in the chair and fell asleep.

Seemed like I had just dozed off, but I was awakened by the

vibrating of my phone in my pocket. Mr. Calvin and Kortlynn were staring at me like I'd done something wrong. Then, I felt it. I wiped the slobber from my chin, as they laughed. "Ha, ha, ha," I said sarcastically.

When I pulled my phone from my pocket, I noticed I'd missed a call from my mama. I stood from my seat and said, "That was my mama. Let me step out and call her back."

"Okay, baby."

I called her back as I was walking out. She answered, "Hello?"

"Hey, baby."

"Hey. What's up? I can hear that something is wrong in your voice."

"They arrested Kerry. They finally caught up with him. Your dad isn't doing well, because he's worried about him, so I have to go bail him out."

"What's going on with Daddy? Do I need to come out there?"

"Please? I just feel bad about going bail him out, knowing he tried to Cain you."

"Cain me?"

"Yeah. Like Cain and Abel in the Bible. Cain killed Abel out of jealousy."

"Mama, it's cool. I just don't have shit to say to him right now."

"I know."

"Okay. Let me tell Kortlynn that I have to leave for a bit. I may bring Daddy back here with me. I have to get us lunch."

"Okay, baby. I'm sorry to inconvenience you."

"It's okay, Ma. I'll be there in a little bit."

"Okay."

Now this shit made me even angrier. Not at my parents but at Kerry. Daddy was already sick and trying to get better, but he couldn't do that if he was stressed out. After walking back inside, I sat next to Mr. Calvin. "Baby, I have to go get my daddy and I'll bring lunch on my way back. They caught up with Kerry and he isn't taking it too well. So, Mama going bail his sorry ass out. Sorry, Mr. Calvin."

He waved his hand as Kortlynn said, "Damn. Okay, baby. I'm sorry."

"Thanks, sweetheart. I'll be back as soon as I can."

"No rush, baby. Be careful."

She grabbed my hand and kissed it. Had a nigga feeling all sensitive and shit. I smiled slightly then bent over and kissed her lips. When I got outside, I put a little pep in my step. I'd driven Kortlynn to the treatment facility, so I was her ride home. After getting in my truck, I called my mama to see if she'd left yet. "Hello?"

"Hey. You left yet?"

"Not yet. I was trying to wait for you to get here."

"Okay. I'll be there in ten minutes."

"Okay."

I ended the call and hauled ass to get there so she could go. I wondered how much his bail was. They should have left his punk ass in jail, though. He did the shit he did because he knew they would always be there for him. They'd always be there, as his safety net, when shit didn't work out. It had always been that way and, now that he was close to forty years old, the shit hadn't changed. Not only was that pathetic, it was embarrassing.

When I got there, Mama was on the porch. I got out my truck to get Daddy to the truck. I kissed my Mama. "How much is his bail?"

"Five grand. The man's family is trying to push the DA to add attempted murder to the charges."

I exhaled and shook my head, then rubbed my hand down my face. Just because I hated seeing my parents spend their money on his bullshit, I briefly thought about giving her half. That thought left me quickly when I thought about how it could've been my ass getting bailed out today. If it would have been, there wouldn't have been a thing my parents could've said to keep me off his ass. I went inside to find my daddy putting on his shoes. "You aight, old man?"

"Yeah."

"I don't know why you let Kerry's shenanigans get to you. I guess, one day, when I have kids, I'll understand."

That last line was just for him. I knew that was what he was going to say, so I beat him to the punch. He looked at me, as he stood. "Well, you better have some kids soon before your soldiers stop swimming."

"Oh, you got jokes, huh? Come on and let's go."

❧

WHEN WE GOT TO THE TREATMENT FACILITY, I WAS HUNGRY AS hell. I'd stopped at Chick-fil-a and got my baby a grilled chicken salad and I got the sandwich. She was doing so well on her diet. She had a doctor's appointment, next month, and I couldn't wait for him to see how well she was doing. When we walked inside, Mr. Calvin's eyes lit up. "Henry Ardoin!"

My dad squinted his eyes. "Calvin Wyatt?"

"Yeah! How are you, man?"

My dad rushed over to him and shook his hand excitedly while Kortlynn and I looked on. She stood and allowed me to sit, so she could sit on my lap. My dad sat on the other side of him and they finally thought we might wanna know how they knew each other. "Years ago, we worked for the railroad together. We were both probably straight out of high school. Who would have known that we would reconnect again this way?" Mr. Calvin explained.

"Yes. Now, I'm glad we've reconnected. I can get my son to drop me off to your house when he's coming to see my daughter-in-law."

Barbara and Henry were something else. Mr. Calvin's eyes widened like there was something we hadn't told him. I rolled my eyes. "They've been calling her that since the first time they met her. There hasn't been any talks of marriage, Mr. Calvin. You'll be the first person I talk to, after Kortlynn and I get to that point."

He nodded his head and smiled. I was glad my dad came, though, because Mr. Calvin seemed to perk up, talking non-stop. Kortlynn and I went outside to eat, since the two of them were in their own world. "It's a small world, huh?"

"Extremely."

"This salad is so good. Thanks, baby," she said, after chewing and swallowing the first mouthful.

"Anytime, baby."

As we ate, I thought about everything my parents had been saying. Kortlynn was the woman I wanted, without a doubt. She was the woman I loved, and I knew, without a shadow of a doubt, that I wanted her to be mine forever. We'd only been together three months, though, and there was no way I'd push her into a forever type of commitment. She liked taking things a little slower than I did. That was okay, though, because I knew how she felt about me.

Chapter Twenty-Five

K ortlynn

"You have every right to feel the way you do."

"Thanks, Serita. I feel bad about shutting my mama out after she told me her truth, no matter how painful it was. I'm going to see her, when I leave from here."

"Just make sure you're mentally and emotionally ready for that. It's only been a couple of days since that revelation. That was a lot to take in. Just continue to look to God for guidance, because He's the wonderful counselor. Okay?"

"I will. I believe He has me covered. Thanks so much, Serita."

"You're welcome."

I left her office and went back to mine to finish the paperwork I was working on, for good. I was so ready to be done with it. My mama had been heavily on my mind, especially after talking to my daddy yesterday. I was tired as hell, too, because I'd stayed on the phone

TRAINING MY HEART TO LOVE YOU

with Zay until late last night. He was about to have a meltdown. When he and his dad had gotten back to China, his brother was at his parents' house still. He said his mama had to stand in front of him to keep him off Kerry.

I could believe that. Zay had been angry about what his brother had tried to do to him since Wednesday. Instead of it getting easier to deal with, it had been festering. It was like Kerry wanted to be there when Zayson got back with their dad. That was crazy as hell to me as well. He had a house to go to. As I finished up the grant paperwork, my phone rang. I just knew it was Zay, but it was Aunt Rose. "Hello?"

"Hey, baby. How are you?"

"I'm good, Aunt Rose. What about you?"

"I'm good. I just wanted to see if you wanted to know who your biological dad is. I have his contact information."

"No, ma'am. He raped my mama, so there's nothing I need to talk to him about. I am going to my mama's house, when I get off, though."

"Well, that's good. You know she really loves you. I know what she said, but when you were little, she was so protective of you. Mary would dress you like a little porcelain doll. If somebody touched your hair wrong, she was on them... quick. To me, that was love. She's looking at it like an obsession instead of love. The way she fell to her knees and hugged you around your legs, says love to me."

"I know. I plan to go over there, today, to talk to her."

"Good. I wish I had known about all of this a long time ago. I was so hard on her, and it just crushes my soul to know that she was going through so much. I stayed with her all night Wednesday. My soul was hurt. Semien and Legend were blowing my phone up."

"Don't be hard on yourself, Auntie. You couldn't help her if she didn't tell you."

"I know, but it doesn't stop me from feeling bad about it. It'll get better, over time. I'm sure of that. I'll let you go, niece. I love you."

"Love you, too."

I ended the call and rested my head in my hands. What Aunt

Rose said made plenty of sense to me and I'd felt that way, once I had time to think. Her words just carried so much weight, they figuratively knocked me to my knees. I'd felt that she hated me at times and her words only amplified that feeling. But, after having time to think, I realized she was hurting and when she lashed out on me or said hurtful things, she was crying out for help. Her entire existence had been affected by this senseless act. I believe because it was someone she knew, it hurt her even more.

After finishing my paperwork, I called Zayson. I hadn't heard from him since this morning. I knew he was trying to deal with his brother's betrayal, as well, plus he had a lot of work to catch up on. He'd taken off and was with me for the whole day, trying to be there for me. Not to mention, Wednesday evening, when he'd catered to me, like never before, and loved me so tenderly. Moments like that, I could literally lay in his arms forever. His phone rang a few times, then it went to voicemail.

He was probably training that horse or practicing with Red. His first rodeo was coming up soon. Their time had been getting better and better, every time they practiced. The quicker they could rope that steer, the better their chances of winning the event at the rodeo. I received a text from him. *I'll call you as soon as I leave Red's house. Love you.*

Just as I figured. He rarely missed my calls and when he did, he was sure to send a text. That was my baby. Perfect, in every way, for me. I suppose I had Legend to thank for that. Adjusting my shirt on my shoulder, I grabbed my purse to head out. I was going to have to go shopping, soon, for more clothes or get some of them altered. I didn't plan on trying to get skinny. I was just trying to be healthy. Hopefully, I'd done enough to get rid of that borderline diabetes, so Zay wouldn't be so hard on me. Although, he'd relaxed, a little, this past week.

After going home to change into my workout gear, I headed to my mother's house. On my way there, Zay called me. "Hello?"

"Hey, baby. Sorry, I couldn't talk earlier. You're still coming out here, right?"

"Of course. I'm gonna be a little late, though, because I'm going to my mama's house. I need to talk to her again and love on her."

"Okay, baby. I'm proud of you."

"Thanks, baby. Aunt Rose asked if I wanted my bio dad's contact information. I told her no. I had no need for that. I'm sure he doesn't know that I exist."

"That has to be tough. You hate him for what he did to your mother, but at the same time, you wouldn't be here otherwise."

"Right. But I don't care about him. He doesn't have a place in my life. He'll only complicate it and bring negative vibes. I can't have his presence disrupting my spirit like that."

"I know, baby. Well, call me when you're on your way. I'm heading home, now, to take a shower."

"Okay. See you later."

I ended the call as I turned into my mother's driveway. Once again, I was trembling, but I believed it was more from emotions that I normally kept on the inside versus the nervousness I was feeling a couple of days ago. Looking in the mirror, I fingered my hair and made sure my lipstick was fresh. That was something I always did before going into my mother's house. Now, I did it more out of habit than any other reason.

When I got out, I pulled up my spandex tights, then pulled down my shirt. Since I was going to work out, I knew my mama wouldn't have an issue with my clothes. Back in the day, tights were forbidden attire. Even now, I tried to be perfect for her. It was engrained in my mind. It was engrained in who I was. Not that it was a bad thing but, in the beginning, it seemed I was living for her. For the past few years, I'd been living for myself, but those practices were still very much a part of who I was.

I walked to the front door and rang the doorbell. Brushing my hair from my face, with my hand, I could see it tremble. When she opened the door, her eyes were wide, and I could see the hope in them. "Hey, Mom."

"Hi, Kort. Come on in."

She stepped aside and I walked through the doorway. After she closed the door, I pulled her in my arms and hugged her tightly. She hugged me back and we stayed that way for a few seconds. When I pulled away, she smiled at me and led me to the sofa. "You want something to drink or eat?"

"No, ma'am. I just wanted to come by and see how you were doing."

"I'm okay. I need to apologize. I think I said some hurtful things to you, and I didn't mean it to sound as harsh as it did. I should've explained myself. I love you, Kortlynn. What I meant was that, because of how I felt, when I looked at you sometimes, it made me feel like I didn't love you. Because I saw him when I looked at you, it made me sick. But I love you. I did then, too. You are innocent in all of this and I'm blessed to have you in my life."

"I understand, Mom. That's why I came, today, to tell you that I understand. I couldn't imagine going through what you went through and having me as a constant reminder of what happened to you. I forgive you for everything and I ask you to forgive my reactions to some things you may have said or done. I saw your behavior as being hateful when actually they were done out of hurt."

"Thank you, Kort. I actually feel better about letting it out. It was holding me hostage. The only person that knew was Calvin. He's been so supportive, even when I pushed him away. That's why I knew that I had to go be with him. This charade we were keeping up wasn't nearly as important as me being there for him. I was actually about to go cook dinner for him."

"I'm glad you're feeling better. Well, I won't hold you."

I stood from my seat and was about to head to the door when she grabbed my hand. "I know you're mad at J'Neka. I couldn't see past my hatred for men and I was so scared someone was going to hurt you, the same way I'd been hurt, even after you were grown. She only did what I asked of her. She would have never disrespected you that way on her own. She does love you, Kort."

"I don't know, Mom. I can forgive her, but we can never have what we once did. No one could ever persuade me to do wrong if I didn't already want to do it anyway. It wasn't hard to persuade her, because it was something she wanted to do. If my friendship meant anything to her, or if she was loyal to me as her cousin, there wouldn't have been anything anyone could have persuaded her to do to hurt me."

"I suppose you're right. At least forgive her for your sanity."

"I have. If I didn't, I was gonna choke the hell out of her. Zayson is more than I could have ever imagined and I'm not about to let anyone try to destroy that."

"About Zayson... I owe him an apology. He seems like a nice guy and I'm glad you found love."

"Thanks, Mom."

I walked to the door and, before I left, I hugged her tightly and kissed her cheek. "Maybe we can have lunch one day next week."

"That would be great. Just let me know when."

I smiled at her, then walked to my car.

AFTER LEAVING MY MAMA'S HOUSE, KNOWING THAT ALL WAS well in my world now, I was in a hurry to get to Zayson. Well, almost everything was well. The situation with J'Neka had been settled but our relationship would never be "well." I wasn't as hurt about that, though. The things she'd said to Zayson, before I got there, let me know how she really felt. I was pretty sure my mother didn't give her a script to go by.

When I got there, I noticed Zayson's mother's car in the driveway. I was sure they were in there talking about his brother. His dad had come to Beaumont, earlier today, to sit with my dad. I was happy they'd reconnected, and I was happy to know that, for the most part, our parents liked each other. I was so glad that Mrs. Barbara hadn't met my mom, before all this, because I was positive they wouldn't have liked one another, especially with the way my mama was treating Zayson. Before I could get to the porch, another car had turned in his driveway. *What was going on?* Zayson rarely had company. I hurried to the door and knocked. When he opened it, his eyes were red. "Hi, baby. What's going on?"

"Mama found Kerry, dead in his house, about two hours ago."

My hand flew to my mouth as he pulled me inside. I hugged him tightly around his waist. "I'm so sorry, baby."

He kissed my head as I eased away from him. "Come, sit down. I'm gonna go in here and see what I can cook."

After he sat, I hugged his parents. Mrs. Barbara was crying already, but she started wailing. I considered myself strong but that yanked the tears right from me. When I got to the kitchen, I didn't find a thing, so I called my daddy. "Hello?"

"Hey, Daddy."

"Hey, baby girl. What's wrong?"

"Zayson's brother was found dead, in his house, a couple of hours ago. I don't know how you're feeling, but it would do Mr. Henry some good to have your support."

"Your mom and I are on our way."

"Can y'all stop to Popeyes or Church's and get some fried chicken." I looked toward the door to see several more people coming in. "A lot of it. I'll pay you back when you get here."

"No need. We'll stop to Popeyes. Let me call it in now."

"Thanks, Daddy."

After talking to them, I called Aunt Rose and then Harper and Shana, so they could tell Legend and Red. They were the only friends of Zayson that I knew. He had more friends, but I didn't know how to contact them. I was almost sure they would find out. Everybody knew everything out here. I went to the couch and he pulled me down on his lap. I noticed that he loved for me to be there. Loosely wrapping my arms around his neck, I kissed his head. When I saw the tear drop from his eye, it hurt like hell. He quickly wiped it. I pulled his head to my chest and asked, "What happened, baby?"

"We don't know yet but, now, I wish I would have forgiven him instead of trying to fight him. I'll never get the opportunity now."

"No. Don't do that." I lifted his head and stared in his eyes. "Don't do that to yourself. You restrained yourself more than you realize. You loved your brother. Don't let anything or anybody make you feel like you didn't. Everything Kerry did, even the things he did against you, you were there for him, whenever he needed you. So, don't allow yourself to feel guilty about a thing. Unfortunately, like the old people say, Kerry made his bed and now he has to lay in it."

He didn't say a word in response to what I said, so I pulled his head back to my chest and held him close. "My parents are on the way with chicken."

"Thanks, baby."

I kissed his head, as I watched more people come in. This was sad and I was praying that Kerry didn't do this to himself.

Chapter Twenty-Six

Z ayson

THE PAST COUPLE OF DAYS HAD BEEN A HUGE BLUR AND THEY all seemed to run together. Kerry was dead and it was tragic to all of us. Regardless of all the shitty things he'd done to me and my parents, we loved him. The biggest thing was that he knew we loved him. So, it came as a shock when they ruled his death a suicide. After investigating, the bruising and burns on his hand was from the kickback of the revolver he'd used to blow his brains out. It also had his prints on it. When he fell to the floor, the revolver had left his hand and ended up under his sofa. It was a selfish way for him to leave, knowing how much we wanted to see him do better. I could only guess that he was embarrassed with the way his life was going. They hadn't charged him with attempted murder, since the guy's wounds weren't as serious as they seemed at first. He probably wouldn't have gotten much time for assault, if any at all, since he didn't have a record.

However, in his death, I chose to focus on the good times we had and not all the recent shit we'd been through. His funeral would be next weekend and, then, we could finally try to move on from this tragedy. My house had been full every day this weekend and my parents had been staying with me. I wanted my daddy close to me. Him having a heart attack from the stress of losing Kerry was all I could think about. Mr. Calvin and Ms. Mary had been coming every day with food and Mr. Calvin was keeping my daddy's spirits up.

Tomorrow was Monday, so Mr. and Mrs. Semien would be coming to keep them company throughout the day. I wasn't sure if Kortlynn was going to work or not, but she had been amazing. I was so glad she was here. While I knew she would have been here this weekend, anyway, she didn't have to be as helpful as she'd been. She'd kept my house clean and helped her parents make sure there was enough food for everyone that came through to offer their condolences. Harper had also kept a good supply of sweets.

Shana and Red had welcomed the birth of their baby boy, a month or so ago, and they brought him over. From the moment my mama held him, it seemed she forgot that she was grieving. Shana let her hold him the entire time they were there. He was gonna have to get used to people calling him lil Red, if his complexion didn't darken any. He looked just like his daddy.

I'd been outside, on my horse, practicing with Red and Legend while Harper, Shana and Kortlynn helped Mrs. Semien cook. My mama watched the boys. Legend and Harper's son was close to a year old and the baby did a lot of sleeping. "I know your mind is occupied, but you roping this shit faster than you did the other day," Legend said.

"Yeah, I think he ready and the rodeo ain't for another three weeks," Red added.

"Yep. I told y'all I would be ready."

"Well, we see nigga!" Legend said, causing me to chuckle.

"What was our time?" I asked.

"Four point six seconds," Legend said.

"Shit, we gotta practice more. I know we can get under four."

They both looked at me like I was crazy, but I had to be sure that this shit profited me. If I was gonna do this, we were gonna have to be amazing, just like they were in their individual events. I was sure Red's time was faster than mine. He could rope the horns from the damn gate. He was setting that shit up perfect for me, most times, but there was a time or two I had to wait on that hop to catch those hind legs. If the hop wasn't there, it was damn near impossible to rope. When Red did a dally, making his left turn, that was when that hop was supposed to happen. "Zay, don't stress, man. We gon' get the time down, but under four... shit we gon' have to be perfect."

"It can be done. If you can bulldog a steer in under four, then we can do this shit in under four."

"Well, shit. Let's do this shit, then. Y'all run it again," Legend said.

If anything, I was doing this shit in memory of my brother. I knew that would push me as hard as I could go. What Kortlynn had said to me Friday evening was spot on. I couldn't keep wallowing in guilt and regret. Kerry and I had disagreements, but that didn't make me love him any less and it surely didn't mean I wanted to see him suffer this fate. So, I could choose to be angry at how he left us, or I could move forward in his memory. I chose the latter.

⚜

RUBBING HER BODY DOWN WITH HER KNATURAL KREATIONS Body Souffle, I whispered in her ear, "Damn, this smells good."

"I know. I have the candle lit, over there, too. They're the same scent."

I smelled my hands. It wasn't terribly feminine, so I might have her order some for me. "What fragrance is this?"

"Lavender Mint."

"You'll order some for me?"

"Already did. It's in my bag."

188

"Well, I guess you think you know me."

"Oh, but I do. From those brown curls on your head to the toenails I just clipped."

"Mmm. Say that shit, baby. Thank you for staying with us all week. The funeral might be hard, tomorrow but, I know, with you by my side, I'll be good."

"Baby, I don't wanna take away room from the family."

"You are family. What do my parents call you? Secondly, half those muthafuckas that been coming here, I ain't seen in years."

I continued rubbing those beautiful, toned thighs and I could feel my body heating up. We couldn't be loud, though, because my parents were still sleeping here. She moaned and I couldn't help but rub her ass. We hadn't had sex all week and I missed her. I got in bed with her and she immediately got up on her knees. When she got in front of me, I knew it was about to be on. I propped my head up on the pillows and watched her kiss the head of my dick and lick down the shaft, lubing it up a little bit. My shit was so hard, the veins looked like they were going to burst through the skin. She eventually lowered her lips on the head, and I wanted to thrust all my shit in her mouth. The pace was killing me. I closed my eyes and waited. Finally, I heard, "Zayson?"

I opened my eyes to see my beautiful queen staring at me. "Can I take my time tonight and show you how much I love and cherish you?"

"I thought you always showed me that shit. But I'm down for whatever you want to do."

Kortlynn giggled then lowered her lips to the head of my dick. My shit was so tender, I couldn't help but intake air at how she was teasing me. I was so ready to glide against her tonsils. That was one of the best feelings in the world. For now, I had to settle for her sucking the head of my dick. It felt like I was about to explode. She finally went lower... slowly, ingesting me one inch at a time, then sliding back up.

This ride was torturous, and I was ready to file charges for cruel and unusual punishment. I closed my eyes, once again, and took in steady breaths until she'd deep throated my shit. She took slow strokes, moaning and leaving her saliva all over me. I opened my eyes to see her hair creating a curtain around what I needed to see. Sitting up, I quickly pulled it up and held it at the top of her head. I found myself grunting with every plunge my dick experienced. My nut was knocking at the door, and I wanted to open it and welcome it inside the walls of her throat, but I needed to mentally prepare to be quiet.

I found myself itching to cum, but not really being able to at this point. I wasn't sure what was going on. Thankfully, I wasn't deflating. "Swallow that dick, baby" I whispered.

She opened her eyes and stared at me, as she sucked. "Fuck, girl. You want this shit?"

Her staring at me was doing the trick. I was glad that it was, because I wouldn't have known how to explain what had happened. Gripping her hair tighter, as she moaned on my dick, I lifted and lowered her head at the pace I desperately needed. Just for a moment, though. When I felt my nut was about to spring out of me like she'd struck oil, I let her go. After a few more strokes, I nut in her mouth, as my body shivered uncontrollably.

After she'd digested every drop, she looked at my flaccid dick and gave me a look of sympathy. Normally after oral sex, he would still be on go. Maybe I was just drained, but I had to at least give my baby one round. Laying her on her back, I slid down her body, as I kissed her in various spots, then landed in the spot that mattered most. It was where I needed to be to drink from the fountain of healing waters.

My dick was rising once again, and I was grateful. I slurped and lapped at her goodness while gripping her thighs. Kort's thighs began trembling, as I lifted her legs, pushing her knees to her sides. Her soft moans and pants let me know that she was enjoying the feeling, so I increased my rhythm, sucking the life out of her clit, as I slid a finger in her ass. She squirmed and I knew her orgasm was coming to greet me. I stroked her asshole like I never had, as she put the pillow over her face. I almost laughed, but I continued what I was doing and, the moment she started to cum, I sat up and slammed my dick into her.

The way she screamed in the pillow was such a fucking turn on. I removed it and kissed her lips, as she continued to cum on my dick. Making my way to her neck, I kissed her softly. "I love you, Kortlynn. I'm never letting you go. I hope you know that."

"I do. I hope you know that I want you to hold on tight. I don't want you to ever let me go, because you letting go would mean that I would have to work extra hard to keep holding on to you. 'Cause I can't let go. Ever."

Damn. I stroked her so slowly and passionately, I couldn't help but verbalize the ultimate satisfaction I was feeling. "Kort, I wanna marry you. I wanna show you how committed I am to us." I closed my eyes, as I felt her pussy gush. "Fuck!" I whispered harshly.

Gently running my hand up her stomach to her chest, then neck, I gripped it gently. Her lips were begging for mine, so I lowered them to hers as she moaned in my mouth, releasing her orgasm. While she rode the wave, I picked up speed and began digging out the pussy, giving it something to remember about this performance. "Kortlynn. You my everything, girl."

"You're my... everything, too."

I latched onto her nipple and gently tugged at it with my teeth, then sucked the life out of it. Her legs began trembling again as she gave up the goods and, this time, she took me down with her. My entire body shivered as I dumped my seed into her womb. One day, that was gonna matter. Because one day, she would be my wife and I'd be dropping these investments to yield a return.

Chapter Twenty-Seven

K ortlynn

THE FUNERAL WAS SO SAD. ZAYSON HAD WORN SHADES, BUT I knew he was crying. His mama had cried loudly, and it caused everyone else to cry. After she'd calmed down, everything else went smoothly. The casket remained closed. Although the funeral home was able to dress his face where you couldn't tell, it would just be too hard on the family to have it open. I'd held Zayson's hand the entire time and I could really feel how much he was hurting. His touch felt heavy and burdened. However, once we'd left for the burial and came back to the Catholic church, for the repast, it had lifted somewhat.

After leaving the repast, we'd gone back to his house, where he said he just wanted to be alone for a little bit. I respected his wishes, because I could imagine how drained he was. Every day, his house had been filled with people. I was also there, so he couldn't really get any alone time, except when he went to the bathroom. He'd stayed in his room for an hour, then the rest of the day, we chose to watch movies and enjoy one another's company.

THE FUNERAL HAD BEEN A WEEK AGO AND I HAD GONE BACK TO work that Monday. Things had been going well with the summer program and their crops were ready to be picked. Zayson would be here after lunch and the girls couldn't wait. They'd enjoyed activities that included fashion design, debate and learned to properly wash and take care of their hair. Serita had gotten beauticians to come in, for two days, last week. She was what this center was missing. She had so much pull in the community. People respected her and were willing to do so much, when she was involved.

As I sat at my desk, I was desperately trying to think about what I wanted for lunch. I didn't bring one from home, today, because I was beat. Meal prepping was the last thing I wanted to do this week. Zayson and I had even taken a day away from one another, to give each other a breather. So, when I left Monday morning, I didn't see him again until Wednesday. Daddy was done with chemo, so I had gone to China to workout with Zayson, while his dad had come to Beaumont to spend time with my daddy. He seemed to be getting stronger and stronger every day. Mama had been spending a lot of time with him. She said he was the only man she'd ever loved, at one point, so hopefully, they could work it out.

My mama and I had gone to lunch and actually enjoyed one another's company. We'd also had another day when we went to lunch with Mrs. Barbara. They seemed to get along well, although, they'd met at a terrible time in Mrs. Barbara's life. Thankfully, she was doing much better, trying to move forward from Kerry's death. So, everything had been going well. I'd even seen J'Neka in Target. I spoke to her like she was a distant cousin, although she seemed like she wanted to say more. She didn't get the chance, though, because

I'd kept walking. I didn't know why she thought she deserved more than a hello, how are you.

Once I'd gotten back from McAlister's Deli, I sat in my office, eating my sandwich with some chips and the best sweet tea I'd ever tasted. Shana and Harper had told me about how good their tea was, and we'd gone there together before. As I ate, there was a knock at my door. Looking at the time, I noticed I was about five minutes past lunch. I opened it to find Zayson standing there with a bouquet of pink tulips.

I smiled at him, then invited him inside. He closed the door, then sat the flowers on a side table, against the wall. I slid my hands up his chest and looped them around his neck, as I softly kissed his lips. "Hey, baby."

"Hey, Kort. How's your day been?"

"It's been okay," I said as I walked around the desk and flopped in my chair to finish my food. "Give me five minutes and I'll be ready."

"That's okay, baby. I was thinking that I should take you out, tonight. Wherever you wanna go, it will be my pleasure to take you there."

"Can we go to Suga's again?"

"Wherever you wanna go, baby."

"Thank you. I appreciate that. I also appreciate this muscle shirt you're wearing. I'm almost sure your lil admirers will appreciate it, too. They are gonna go crazy over these tattoos. I already know," I said, as I shook my head slowly and took a sip of my tea.

"At least I didn't wear gray pants."

"You ain't crazy."

Zayson laughed as I stood from my seat. Pulling me in his arms, he laid a kiss on me that instantly flooded my panties. "Damn. What did I do to deserve that?" I asked breathlessly.

"Just being you. I really appreciate you being there for me, baby. I know you keep saying I don't have to thank you," he said, when he'd noticed my facial expression. "But, I do, baby. You love me so hard and so strong, that I can't help but be in awe with how big your heart is. You encouraged me, gave me sound advice, and took care of me. Baby, that was huge to me and I'll never forget it."

I smiled at him, then kissed his lips, once again, and led him outside to his hot in the pants fans.

WHEN WE WALKED IN SUGA'S, THERE WAS A LIVE BAND PLAYING. I was too excited, because I loved live music, especially jazz and soul music. Robert Glasper and Terrace Martin were a couple of my favorites. We were seated rather quickly, and I immediately began grooving to the sounds while Zayson smiled at me. I couldn't wait to eat the stuffed pork chops. They'd been calling my name since I'd mentioned Suga's.

After giving our drink orders, I had to stand and groove to the music. Zayson sat there and laughed at me, the entire time. He looked extremely happy and that made me happy. I sat briefly when the waitress brought our drinks, so I could order my main course. Then, I was right back on my feet, having an amazing time. Once they took a short break, I joined Zayson back at our table. He'd already gotten a refill. "Thirsty?"

"Shit, I was parched. Watching you dance, all that time, had me sitting here with my mouth open. Shit was drier than the Sahara Desert."

We laughed and talked about how we would have fun with Legend, Red, Harper and Shana, tomorrow, after they practice. We'd had a great time at Red's house, the last time. This time, it would be at Legend's house, in Liberty. When they brought out the food, the conversation stopped. My mouth was literally watering at the sight of those pork chops. It came with some greens and crawfish and sausage cornbread dressing.

Zayson had also gotten the stuffed pork chops but got cajun cabbage and garlic mashed potatoes as his sides. After a good thirty minutes, our plates were clean. We looked up at one another and laughed at how quickly we'd eaten, and practically had done it in silence. When the waitress came to see if we wanted dessert, Zay ordered ice cream and a brownie for us to share. I didn't know where I was gonna put it. I was so stuffed already. As we sat, holding hands and talking, the band began playing "Happily Ever After" by Case. I used to love that song! "Come on, Zay. Let's dance."

He smiled, then stood and escorted me to an open area. His eyes stayed on me, and the moment was so intense, chill bumps had popped up on my flesh. He dug in his pocket and when Case sang *in my hand there was a ring*, he took a ring out of his pocket. My heart quickened and my nerves were on edge. As Case sang, *so I asked you would you do me the honor of being my wife*, Zay went down on his knee and licked his lips, as the whole restaurant paused. "I love you, Kortlynn Denise Hebert. You don't have to marry me tomorrow, next month, or even next year. But, please, just tell me you will, one day. I don't wanna live this life without you, because I won't be living. You came in my life and stole my heart... my soul. So, without you, I'll die, baby."

Oh, my God! My heart felt like it was gonna beat out of my chest, as I stared at him. Something that rarely happened, had happened. The tears were streaming down my face, at his gesture and words, and I couldn't make them stop. My hand was trembling in his, as he continued, "Like the song said, will you do me the honor of being my wife?"

It felt like I was hyperventilating. There wasn't a doubt in my mind about where this man stood in my life. I quickly nodded my head. "Yes, Zayson. God, yes."

He slid this beautiful, mixed chocolate and white diamond ring on my finger. God, it was gorgeous. The band was rose gold and I almost couldn't take my eyes off it. I wasn't a materialistic person, but damn! Zayson stood while I was admiring the ring. I looked up at him. "Is this real?"

"It's very real, baby."

His face was so serious. The applause around us brought me back to my senses. I threw my arms around him and kissed his lips. I'd been so wrapped up in him I never noticed that our parents were all here, along with Legend, Harper, Red, Shana and Aunt Rose. I laughed loudly as they whistled and applauded. Zayson finally smiled and, when he did, I slid my hands up his chest to his face and pulled him to me. My lips interlocked with his and I didn't spare none of the nasty shit I gave him when we were alone. He yanked my hips to his and kissed me a little longer, then pulled away from me. "Baby, we can't give away all our nasty ass secrets. You 'bout to make me throw you on top of this damn piano and have this band accompany our melody."

I laughed, as he led me to our seats. The family was seated in the back of the restaurant, which was how I didn't see them. "Zayson. I can't believe you did this."

"I told you, several times, that I wanna marry you. I ain't playing wit'chu, girl."

I giggled, then looked at my ring again. "I see, baby. Shit. This ring is beautiful."

"You deserve all the beauty it has to offer, plus some. As my woman, Kort, you ain't gotta want for nothing. I know you ain't into all that expensive bullshit but, whatever you want, I got'chu."

"Same for you, Zay. Whatever."

I licked my lips and he smiled at me, as the waitress brought our dessert. She sat it on the table. "You two are really a beautiful couple. Congratulations."

"Thank you," we said in unison.

When she left, Zay spooned some ice cream and brought it to my lips. "Back to what you were saying, Kort. You said whatever, right?"

"Mmm hmm." After swallowing my ice cream, I continued, "Whatever, Zayson."

"Aight. So, after your lease is up, I want you to move to China with me."

"In three months. I'll be there, big daddy."

"See, why you wanna start that shit in here?" He lowered his voice and leaned in closer to me. "My dick hard as fuck right now. You want all the women in here to get a glimpse of yo' shit?"

I licked my lips, then ate the brownie he'd spooned for me. After clearing my mouth of the delicious dessert, I gently rubbed his face. "No, I don't, but I can't help it. You so sexy, I just can't resist all this shit you offering me, right now. If you picked me up and sat me on this table, I'd spread eagle for you, right here, in front of all these people."

Zayson's eyebrows lifted, then he pulled out his wallet and sat two hundred-dollar bills on the table. "Come on, girl. Let's get the fuck outta here before I take you up on that."

"What about our family?"

"Them muthafuckas grown. They all married already, so they better know what the deal is. Let's go, before I embarrass yo' sexy ass."

Chapter Twenty-Eight

Z ayson

"You got everything? This three-slant and a large gon' be packed to the gills!"

We were leaving for the rodeo in Fairfield. Kortlynn and I would follow behind Red and, when we got there, we would sleep in his trailer. He had three slants for three horses and the living quarters was huge, which was why it was called a large. Three-slant and a large. He'd traded in his 2010 trailer, when he inherited all that money from his deceased grandparents and got a 2019 Bison. That bitch was loaded and had privacy doors on all the beds. This shit was gon' be rocking tonight, especially if we won. After I loaded our luggage in the trailer, I closed the door. "That's everything. Thanks, man."

It had been a week since I'd proposed to my baby and, although I'd played that shit cool, I was nervous as fuck. When she said she wanted to go to Suga's, I called ahead to put some things in motion. They usually had a band on the weekends, so I knew exactly what I would do. I'd purchased a ring, for her, the same day my mama found my brother dead in his home. My intent was to propose then, but, after finding out my brother was dead, it derailed my plans. But it gave me time to put together something special for her.

The time she took with me, caring for me and my family, touched my heart in ways that made me want to do the most for her. And, that was what I planned to do, for the rest of my life. She'd come in my life and disrupted shit, made a nigga all sensitive and wanting to wife her. But she was definitely worth all that. I got in my truck, ready to hit the road, with the love of my life. "You ready to show them how China, Texas do things?"

"Hell, yeah, baby girl. They gon' be fearing Red and Zay after tonight. You feel me?"

"Yep. I can't wait to celebrate wit'chu, after y'all sweep shit up."

I chuckled, as she licked her lips. She was so damn nasty and I liked that shit. We were rubbing off on each other, too. I found myself speaking correct English more often, and she was getting a lil hood, country swag to her. She was getting plenty of hood, country swag put in her, too. People saw a nigga on a horse, or at a rodeo, and thought he was soft. Shit, we were as hood as the niggas living in the hood. We just had an added component to our personalities because of where we grew up. "Well, baby, you know we gon' be in Red's trailer. We can't have that shit rocking. You know how we get."

"I can almost guarantee that their nasty asses gon' be fucking, too. So, ain't nobody gon' be worried about us."

"Well, damn, girl! I ain't gon' keep the dick from you. Bring down that hostility in your voice. Big daddy sorry."

She laughed loudly and I laughed with her, as she grabbed my hand. Looking at that rock on her left hand made my heart swell. Just like I saw life, love and the world in her, she saw that same shit in me. She trusted me to take care of her, and that was exactly what I was gon' do. We were both old school, in a sense, and I didn't want her to have to worry about how much money she was making, as long as she was doing what she loved. If everything went well today, Serita could decide to make her a fucking volunteer, and she'd be able do that.

By the time we got to Conroe, my shit was throbbing. Kortlynn had been teasing me, and shit, for the past hour. I had to be leaking pre-cum. It was insane, because it was like we could never get enough. We'd fucked early this morning, before we left, and here we were, fiending for the shit like we hadn't seen each other in weeks. Once we got on IH-45 North, and had gotten in a good groove driving, she reached over to my crotch and unzipped my pants. "Look, man. You pull his ass out of his sleeping quarters, you better be ready to give him some neck action."

She smiled, licked her lips and unbuckled her seatbelt. Thank God for dark tinted windows. I lifted my arm and rested it across the back of the seat. When she pulled my dick out, the head was glistening with precum, begging for her attention. She licked her lips again, as she stared at it. "Damn, he wants me, huh?"

"He *needs* you, baby. You gon' give him what he need?"

"Mmm hmm," she said right before wrapping her lips around it and going straight for the gusto. No more teasing, no more playing, baby girl was on her fucking job. I almost closed my damn eyes. Moving my arm from the back of the seat, I grabbed her hair and enjoyed the shit she was doing to me. "Fuck, girl. Shit!"

I wanted to pull over and fuck the shit out of her, but I'd never hear the end of that shit from Legend and Red. She applied extra suction to it, and I damn near lost the mobility of my legs. Her head bobbed up and down quickly, pulling my nut out of me, fast and furiously. "Baby, I'm about to cum."

She grabbed my nut sack and I bust so hard, the truck swerved. Kort swallowed all my kids and was still sucking the shit, begging for more, as I squirmed in my seat. "Shit, Kort!"

She finally let it go, then sat back in her seat and took a black silk-looking bag from her purse. She put her feet up on the dash, then pulled out a dildo. "Yo! What you finna do, girl?"

"Well, you can't fuck me, right now, so I have to fuck myself."

Before I could respond, my phone rang. I answered it on the Bluetooth. "Hello?"

"Yo, you alright? We saw you swerve. You not sleepy, huh?" Legend asked.

"Naw. Yo' cousin tripping."

"Aww, shit. I don't wanna hear no more. Bye, nigga."

I chuckled, as he ended the call, then looked at my fiancée as she moved her panties to the side, her skirt at her waist, and pushed that rubber dick in my sanctuary. I bit my bottom lip as she moaned. "As soon as I get a chance, I'm gon' fuck you up so good. You ain't gon' have no energy to pull no shit like this, on the way back."

She started fucking herself slowly, then pulled that shit out and sucked her juices from it. My dick was hard, all over again, and, if I had to fuck her as soon as we got to Fairfield, in this truck, that was what would happen. Kortlynn pushed it back inside of her and fucked herself fast and hard until she came all over my fucking leather seats. I wanted to pull over and lick all that shit up. "I can't believe you just wasted all that good shit on the seats."

When she caught her breath, she said, "Well, you could always suck it off here."

I frowned. "You done lost yo' got damn mind if you think I'm finna suck a fucking dick."

She laughed loud as hell, then sucked that shit clean and put it back in her bag. "I swear yo' ass is nasty. You kept that shit hidden, too. Now that I'm about to wife you up, you tryna kill me with these surprise revelations."

She laughed again. "Shut up, Zay! You didn't think I was too nasty when I was sucking that nut up out'chu."

I was quiet as hell, trying to hold in my laugh. "Why you turning red, Zay?"

That was it. I laughed hard as hell. "You know I like that nasty shit, girl. Lady in the streets and a freak in the sheets."

JUST AS PLANNED, WHEN WE GOT TO FAIRFIELD, I KNELT ON THE floor of my truck in front of Kortlynn and fucked the shit out of her. The whole truck was smelling like that good shit. I was gonna have to leave my windows down for a minute. When we got out the truck, Legend was frowning and Red had a goofy ass look on his face. "What?"

We walked away from the ladies and Legend said, "Pussy gon' be there. Let's handle business first."

I frowned at him until Red said, "All the times y'all almost fucked in the backseat of my truck with me and Shana in the front? Nigga, shut up."

Legend laughed as we made our way to the registration office to check in. I thought his ass was serious at first. While we were all friends, I was closer to Red. So, I didn't quite know all of Legend's mannerisms yet, but I was learning. Red would be steer wrestling, first, and his wife, Shana, would be hazing for him. It would be her first rodeo since she had the baby. Then, two events later, we would be doing our thing. Legend's event, bull riding, was always the last event.

As we walked back to the trailer, with our registration numbers, I heard somebody say, "Got damn! What events y'all in?"

The three of us turned toward the woman. I was about to walk the hell off without answering her ass, but Red said, "Steer wrestling, team roping and bull riding. So, stay and enjoy the show."

"I sure in the fuck will."

I rolled my eyes and we walked off. "Keep on entertaining them buckle bunnies and Shana gon' fuck you up," Legend said.

"I just answered her question."

"Uh huh. You better keep yo' friendly ass to yourself," I added.

Legend laughed and Red and I joined him. "What's so funny?" Shana asked, as we got back to the trailer.

The three of them were getting Harper's setup from the trailer.

She worked all these rodeos, pulling in money and orders for her pastry business. "Uh... none of your business," Legend said.

She shot daggers at him with her eyes and Red raised his hands and went inside the trailer. When we all got inside, Legend looked at him and said, "Yo' whooped ass."

I laughed, as Harper came inside. Legend quickly made his way to her and kissed her lips. "You need help, baby?" he asked her.

Red and I laughed loudly as I said, "We all whooped. Might as well accept that shit."

Time seemed to fly by, as we sat in the trailer relaxing. Red was getting ready for his event and I was doing my best to stay calm. It was hard as hell, with this nigga blasting Tupac, Tru and everybody else that got a nigga ready for war. Legend was just laughing at his ass while he smoked a blunt. Harper and Kortlynn were out selling treats. Since Shana would be hazing for Red, Kort had agreed to help Harper.

Legend and I followed Red and Shana down to the arena and we would just sit at the back of the chute to watch them get down. They made a perfect team and I knew Red was glad to have her back. The announcer was sure to welcome her back. I looked around the arena, taking everything in. It had been years since I'd been on this side of the events. Before long, it was Red and Shana's turn to go. *"Ladies and gentlemen! Red and Shana Anderson have reunited, and it feels so good! She had that cute lil replica of Red and now they're ready to claim the title together, as a team again. So, y'all readyyyyy? Let's go!"*

Red's horse was antsy as always, but when he nodded, the steer was released, and he and Shana took off. Watching Red wrestle that steer to the ground made me miss competing. However, I knew I couldn't risk getting hurt. I narrowly escaped the last time. Sliding off that horse wasn't as easy as it looked, especially at such a fast pace. Red flipped that shit over so fast, I almost missed it. Shana did a fist pump and screamed, as she made her way back. *"They showed us*

how it's done! That's why he's a world champion at a time of three point two!"

I shook my head, slowly, as I applauded. That nigga was a beast. I just hoped we could get under four seconds in our event. Four seconds was average. I wanted us to be amazing, just like that. It wasn't like either of us were amateurs. We'd been in this shit a while. Legend and I walked out the arena and met Red and Shana, as they jumped around. "That's what the fuck I'm talking about nigga!" Legend yelled at him.

Red was the last wrestler, so he won his event by point four seconds. He picked Shana up and spun her in a circle, while she laughed. It was time for me to calm down, now, and I think Legend could see I was nervous. "You wanna smoke? That's how I keep calm."

"Naw. Ganja makes my ass delusional, so I stay away from that shit."

He laughed. "Big as yo' ass is, you can't handle the dro?"

I laughed with him. "Hell, naw. But I'm finna go next to my baby. She always manages to calm me down."

"Well, do that. Harper does the same for me."

I nodded and walked off to find her, while they blasted the Zydeco music, getting ready for the next event. When I got to Harper's booth, baby girl was busy. I stood motionless, watching her handle business. She was so damn beautiful. When she noticed I was watching her, she smiled at me. After she was done with her customer, she ran to me and hugged me. "How did Red do?"

"He won, baby girl."

"That's awesome. I wish I would have gotten to see him."

She ran her hands along my cheeks. "You okay? You look nervous."

"I am, a lil bit. Can you cum calm me down?"

"You don't even have to ask that. I'll sex you into euphoria. Come on."

Harper smirked at us, as Kort led me to Red's trailer and fucked me into a state of euphoria, just like she said.

❦

"LADIES AND GENTLEMEN, WE HAVE A FRESH TEAM TONIGHT! Red Anderson has teamed up with horse trainer, Zay Ardoin, for this event! They're hoping to create some magic here, tonight. I believe it can probably be done, but that has yet to be seen."

I was nervous as shit. Even after Kort had rode my ass into the sunset. I was relaxed, at first, but the minute our event started, the nerves were back. I sat on my horse and closed my eyes, praying that we did well. I wanted this shit to pop off like now. Taking deep breaths, I clenched my rope and held my horse, Hitman, back. I'd named him Hitman because, if the nigga felt even slightly threatened, he'd attack a human. I whispered, "I'm doing this in memory of you, Kerry."

"So, let's see what they got! Let's get ready!"

I looked over at Red and he gave the head nod. When that steer was released, that nigga threw that rope quick as hell, as we ran out the box. When he did a dally, and that steer jerked left, I threw my rope just as quickly and hooked those hind legs. The announcer was having a fit, as I allowed slack in my rope to release the steer's legs. *"What did we just see?! This has to be close to the record time! Red and Zay didn't come to play. And, whoa!!! Their time is three point nine! It was close to breaking the record of this arena, which was a three point eight!"*

Red and I rode to the back gate and one of the guys working the rodeo pulled his rope off the horns of the steer. We then rode to the back of the arena and tied up our horses, barely able to contain ourselves. "I knew you could do this shit!" Red yelled.

We hugged each other then headed around the arena to see our ladies waiting for us, along with Legend. When Kort made eye contact with me, she ran to me and I picked her up, spinning her around in her ruffled skirt and boots. "Baby, y'all did that so fast, I barely saw it! Congratulations!"

"Thank you, baby. But we don't know if we've won yet."

"Regardless, y'all did an awesome job."

She kissed my lips, as Red yelled, "The steer didn't wanna play! One more to go!"

He was watching the teams after us. When the steer was released, he decided he didn't want to run. So, they just lost out and didn't get a time. I always thought that deserved a redo, but rules were rules. We stood patiently waiting for the next team to go. My baby was so excited, she could barely stay still. I knew she didn't understand everything that was going on, but, because I was involved, she was excited. That made me love her even more. The last team seemed to have done well, but when we heard the announcer say their time was four point whatever, we started celebrating before he could finish.

People had gathered around us and were celebrating as well. When we finally calmed down, I noticed Legend was gone. "Yo, where did Legend go?"

"He works better when he's calm. So, he went to the trailer to smoke and you'll see Harper make her way over there in a minute," Shana said, as she went to the pastry booth.

"I guess Legend and I are alike, when it comes to that," I said to Kortlynn. "You wanna watch the rest of the rodeo or are you gonna stay with the ladies?"

"I wanna be wherever you are, right now."

I grabbed her hand and went to get seats in the arena, as everyone shook my hand, congratulating me. Kortlynn was all smiles. After we sat, I said, "So, this here competition, just won me five grand and a belt buckle."

Kortlynn's eyes widened. "Are you serious?"

"Yep."

"Is that what every rodeo pays?"

"No. Some pay more, some pay less. It just depends on the size of the rodeo and who's promoting it."

"Wow!"

My thoughts exactly. I guess I would be doing this shit permanently, since I knew how good we were.

We'd been sitting here, watching all the events. I had to explain quite a bit to Kortlynn, but I didn't mind. When we'd finally got to the bull riding, she sat at the edge of her seat. When the first guy got bucked off and landed on his back, she looked at me with worried eyes. "Don't worry. Legend is a beast. You gon' see."

Kortlynn had seen Legend ride before, but it was a much smaller rodeo and the bulls didn't seem as aggressive. She watched the next rider get bucked off and I could feel her nervousness. I grabbed her hand and rubbed it, trying to calm her down. Watching bull riding can be quite stressful when there's someone you love competing. Legend was rider number five. When he slid down on the bull, it started bucking, while behind the gate. I watched Red help him get situated, then the gate swung open. Kortlynn sat with her hands clasped together, like she was praying, resting her mouth against them.

The bull made twists and turns, as Legend held on for dear life, spurring the shit out of that bull. When the buzzer sounded, the announcer went crazy, as Legend dismounted and ran to the fence to wait for his score. ***"The living Legend has a score of ninety point six! He's forever showing us how to get it done!"***

I stood and applauded and Kortlynn followed suit. I grabbed her hand and led her out of the stands, so we could go down and celebrate and accept our winnings. When we got down there, we congratulated Legend and Red said, "We done came to Fairfield and swept this shit up!"

We laughed, as I pulled my baby in my arms and kissed her lips. She hugged me tightly around my neck and I felt the love emanating from her. We all headed to the dirt to receive our winnings. Red had received his first, then, when I joined him for our team roping winnings, the announcer asked what motivated me to where I did so well. I looked at Kortlynn and said, "The love and support of my fiancée, Kortlynn Hebert, and the memory of my brother, Kerry Ardoin."

After he handed me my buckle and my check, I gestured for Kortlynn to come take a picture with me. She ran to me and made sure that ring made the picture as well. I chuckled, as I wrapped my arms around her. "Girl, you everything I didn't even know I wanted."

"Uh huh. Show me in the trailer, tonight, big daddy."

"Yo' nasty ass. Don't worry. I'm gon' put this shit to you so good, you gon' be telling Legend, Red, Shana and Harper all our damn business."

She frowned, trying to figure out what I meant. "You gon' be in there screaming out what I'm doing to you."

She laughed and slapped my arm. "I love you, Zay, and, for the record, you're everything I wanted that I didn't think existed."

"Well, damn, baby. I'm right here in the flesh for you to enjoy."

Epilogue

ortlynn
Three months later...

"I LOVE BEING HERE WITH YOU, EVERY NIGHT, ZAY."

"Shit, I more than love it. I get to dig all up in them walls every morning and every night. Shit can't get better."

I giggled, as Zay pulled me close to him. I'd moved in last week and put most of my things in storage until I could decide what to do with them. The past three months had been amazing. Daddy had been doing well and gaining weight. I was so happy because things didn't look so good, at one point. My mama had been spending a lot of time with him and I was just waiting on the day for them to tell me they were a couple.

Zayson's parents were doing a lot better, coping with the death of Kerry. It had been hard for them and, after a couple of weeks, they had come back to Zayson's house to stay for a little while just so they could be close to Zay. It was like being close to him was therapeutic for them, in a way. He was extremely sensitive to whatever his parents needed from him and I couldn't be prouder of the man I loved.

Zay had been to three more rodeos, with Red, and they had won first place in all three. They were unstoppable and I was extremely proud of him. I'd helped Harper and Shana at the pastry booth until Red and Zay's event, then I would go back until Harper shut it down for the night. She always did that right before Legend's bull riding event. We'd all gotten extremely close and I couldn't pray for better friends. Zay was even thinking about competing in calf roping, which would be an individual event.

Integrity had been doing well. Serita had been working the shit out of her PR. We'd been getting in so many donations and we'd also been approved for another grant. I couldn't be happier, because I loved my job. Teaching young girls how to love themselves and be respectable young women was something that meant a lot to me. While my mother had her flaws, she always taught me to love and respect myself. While her intentions for me not dating may have been all screwed up, it still taught me something.

I'd gone to my doctor's appointment and he was surprised to see I'd lost forty pounds. I was standing at two hundred pounds even. This size was workable for me, but I wanted to lose at least five more pounds, just so I could be out of the two hundreds. I'd also began planning our wedding. It would be intimate with only our family and close friends in attendance, but I wanted it to be extremely elegant and beautiful. Shana and Harper had agreed to be in the wedding and Serita's sister, Shannon, would be doing our decorations.

Harper was gonna bake my wedding cake. I knew her sweets were amazing, so it was a no-brainer to have her do it. We were having a March wedding, so we still had five months until the big day. I was so anxious. Harper and Shana had come with me, my mama, Aunt Rose and Mrs. Barbara to find my dress. It was so gorgeous and I knew it was the perfect dress before I even tried it on. The bridesmaids had already gotten fitted for their dresses as well. So, we were only waiting on time to pass.

I never thought I would find my forever, and this soon. There was still a chance for me to have kids. I told Zay I wouldn't mind having a house full. He promised me I would change my mind after the first one. He was probably right. At thirty-two years old, and not having a boyfriend, I figured it would take me forever to get to this point in my life and, not even a year later, we were about to become one. How crazy was that? Zayson was everything I wanted. It was like God took note of everything I desired, then dropped Zay off at Integrity and said, "Here you go, Kortlynn. Enjoy."

I snuggled in Zayson's arms and did just that... enjoyed the feeling of being in a perfect love.

The End

Afterword

From the Author

I hope you enjoyed this country love story! These characters were talkative, and I was begging them to be quiet. They were like, *naw, Mo. You gon' tell this story like we give it to you.* LOL There's also an amazing playlist, on iTunes, for this book under the same title that includes some great R&B tracks to tickle your fancy and a Zydeco tune, if you aren't familiar with the genre. Please keep up with me on Facebook (@authormonicawalters), Instagram (@authormonicawalters) and Twitter (@monlwalters). You can also visit my Amazon author page at www.amazon.com/author/monica.walters to view my releases. Also, subscribe to my webpage for updates! https://authormonicawalters.wixsite.com/mysite.

For live discussions, giveaways and inside information on upcoming releases, join my Facebook group, Monica's Romantic Sweet Spot at https://bit.ly/2P2lo6X.

Coming up:

Please register to meet me, and some amazing authors, on October 5, 2019 at the Houston Loves Books event at www.

houstonlovesbooks.com! Paperbacks will be on deck and waiting to be signed, just for you.

I will also be in Memphis, November 2-3, 2019, for BLP's first meet and greet! Come meet the #girlgang at the BLP Winter Wonderland! Register at Bit.ly/BLPWW19. We look forward to seeing you there!

CPSIA information can be obtained
at www.ICGtesting.com
Printed in the USA
LVHW111449011119
636084LV00003B/390/P